A GOOD BAD IDEA NOVEL

ARIELLA ZOELLE

Copyright © 2020 A.F. Zoelle/Ariella Zoelle

Published by Sarayashi Publishing

www.ariellazoelle.com

All rights reserved.

This is a work of fiction. Names, characters, places, and incidents are products of the author's imagination or used fictitiously. Any resemblance to actual persons, living or dead, is purely coincidental. All products and brand names are registered trademarks of their respective holders/companies.

This book or any portion thereof may not be reproduced or used in any manner whatsoever without the express written permission of the publisher except for the use of brief quotations in a book review.

Cover Design by Cate of Cate Ashwood Designs

Editing by Pam of Undivided Editing

Proofreading by Sandra of One Love Editing

Layout by Ariella of Sarayashi Publishing

ISBN: 978-1-7324473-8-7

Author's Note

The **Good Bad Idea** series can be read in any order. However, if you would like to see where Callum's story began, please refer to **Love Means More**.

Dedication

For all of you who find comfort in cute and sweet fluff, this one is definitely for you.

Welcome to Sunnyside!

Immerse yourself in the world of interconnected series set in the fictional town of Sunnyside

Full of cute sweetness and sexy fun, every story ends with a satisfying HEA and no cliffhangers. Since all of the following series are set in the same town, you can expect to see cameos of your favorite characters! The books are funny, steamy, and can be read in any order.

To access the Sunnyside universe reading order guide, please visit www.ariellazoelle.com/sunnyside

Chapter One

CALLUM

I MIGHT BE the only person in the world whose favorite day of the week was Monday. But there was something so exciting about the promise of a brand new week, where anything was possible. I loved my job as Xander Dandridge's personal assistant, so I practically skipped to work every morning.

Saying hello to everyone as I made my way through the office, I sat down at my desk and got settled to start the workday. As my computer booted up, Xander approached with coffee in hand. He never started a morning without it.

Since he was so handsome and kind, more than half of the employees had a crush on him. His features were delicate, with high cheekbones and elegant eyebrows. I hadn't even known it was possible for eyebrows to be elegant until I met him. They made his green-hazel eyes more striking. The emerald-colored shirt he wore under his black suit also brought out the color in them.

"Good morning, Xander!"

He smiled at my enthusiasm. "Morning. Are you doing well?"

"Always! What about you?"

"I'm great," he answered. "Rhys is coming back today, so I can finally start making some headway on a few things that need his attention."

"I'll let him know you're looking for him when he comes in."

Xander lifted his coffee to me in a toast. "Thanks, I appreciate that."

After he walked back to his office, I set about getting ready to start the day. I was glad Rhys was returning. He had been away on a business trip to Italy that he had extended into a vacation with his husband, Lucien.

Since I had grown up in a religious Irish Catholic family in Dublin, I hadn't met any married gay couples before them. They were like fairy-tale princes living happily ever after. Their marriage was beautiful, and I enjoyed seeing them interact whenever Lucien visited the office. There was so much love between them, and I couldn't help but be envious.

Because I had been so scared of Da finding out I was gay, I had lived deep in the closet of denial back in Ireland, making it impossible for me to date anyone. I had been in love with my best friend,

Gregory, but he gave me a black eye when he found out about my crush. The blow from his fist hadn't hurt as much as losing him afterward.

I had moved on since then, but even after living in Sunnyside for almost six months, I had yet to go out on a single date with a guy. My new friends had offered to set me up, but it was too intimidating to accept their offer. Because I was so inexperienced with dating and love, I worried I would humiliate myself. Logically, I understood that going out with someone was how to get experience. However, it was difficult to overcome my natural shyness and conviction that I would screw things up royally.

I had barely gotten accustomed to swearing freely. My parents instilled in me from a young age to never blaspheme by cursing or taking the Lord's name in vain. But now that I was constantly around Brody, Augie, Felix, and his friends, it was something I had grown more comfortable with. I found it a weirdly comforting break from my past, almost like it was evidence I had broken free from everything that used to hold me back.

Cursing verbally still didn't come to me naturally. However, based on the amount of times the word "fuck" crossed my mind recently, I suspected that would change after a few more months of living in America. It was one thing to do it around my friends and at home, but I refused to do it at work. It went against my need to have consistently polite manners that Ma drilled into me.

"Hey, Callum!"

I turned at the sound of my name and smiled when I saw Rhys approaching. Like Xander, Rhys was exceptionally attractive. It was enough to make me wonder if there was something in the water cooler that caused everyone to look so good. He had chiseled cheekbones and a strong jaw, with beautiful gray-blue eyes. His sandy-blond hair was usually a little mussed, but in a charming way.

"Welcome back!" I was genuinely glad to see him. The office was always more fun when he was there to liven things up. Our company funded technology startups, but Rhys's presence kept everything from feeling too serious. "How was Italy?"

He leaned against my desk counter. "It was *amazing*! It was almost like a second honeymoon."

As in love as Rhys was with Lucien, it didn't surprise me that was the part he commented on first. "That's great."

"The hotels and restaurants you found for us were incredible. We wouldn't have had nearly as nice of a time if it weren't for you."

I puffed up a bit from the praise, happy to know that I had made his trip with his husband special. "I'm so glad you liked everything."

"To show my appreciation, I brought you back something." He dug in his messenger satchel and pulled out a beautiful iridescent cellophane bag stuffed with colorful treats. "Since you share my sweet tooth, I thought you'd enjoy these Italian candies."

It touched me that he would bring me anything at all. "Thank you so much! That's very kind of you. I'm sure I'll love them."

He took out a small, flat box wrapped with purple metallic foil paper trimmed with gold ribbon and held it out to me. "I also got you this."

"But the candy was already more than enough!" When he gestured for me to take it, I accepted. After removing the wrapping paper, it shocked me to see Gio Zapfirino's logo on the lid. The famous Italian fashion designer created not only beautiful clothes, but also incredible bow ties. Both were way too far out of my price range to own. Even the cheapest plain black bow tie was eight hundred dollars. I enjoyed looking at them online and dreaming about adding one to my bow tie collection someday.

I took off the lid and gasped at the sight of three Italian silk Zapfirino bow ties in the box. One featured a purple-and-yellow floral paisley. My jaw dropped at the rainbow ombre print one, trimmed on the edges and center with iridescent glitter. The pastel blue one with sparkling pink rhinestones was the most stunning of them all. I didn't understand how I was holding a box filled with thousands of dollars' worth of silk that somehow belonged to me. The luxury was on an extraordinary level that was impossible to fathom.

It took several tries before I could make words come out in my shock. "T-t-this is too much! I don't deserve—"

He talked over me to insist, "Yes, you do. In the past three months, you've been an enormous help to me and Xander both by making our lives easier. You eagerly volunteer for projects, and no matter what's going on, you always have a smile on your face. Your bow ties brighten everyone's day, so this is the perfect gift for you that you absolutely deserve. Think of it as one for every month you've made a difference here."

Reaching out to the rainbow-colored one with trembling fingers, it was the softest thing I had ever touched. I was almost moved to tears. It was the nicest and most thoughtful present I had received in my life. I stared up at him and hoped he could tell how grateful I was. "Rhys, I can't thank you enough. This means the world to me. *Wow*."

"You're welcome, Callum. I assume Xander wants to see me?"

I nodded, still finding it hard to form words in my emotional state.

"Excellent, I'll go see him and get caught up on what I need to do." He left with a wave.

Unable to believe that he had gifted me a box of treasures, I needed to touch them to make sure they weren't just a figment of my imagination. I picked up the bow tie with the pink rhinestones, which glittered as they reflected the light. It was officially the fanciest thing I owned. Whenever I thought things couldn't get any better, life surprised me again.

I wanted to continue admiring them, but I also needed to start my workday. Putting it back, I closed the lid. Even after I started my project, my gaze kept darting over to the box to make sure it hadn't disappeared, because it was too good to be true.

MY MORNING FLEW BY, bringing lunchtime before I realized time passed. I only noticed when I heard a cheery "Hey, Callum!"

Turning in my chair, I noticed Jules heading my way. He was Xander's best friend, who visited him for lunch sometimes. Friendly, blond, blue-eyed, and handsome, he was the embodiment of what I imagined Americans to be before moving to Sunnyside. He was jovial and always quick to joke. I looked forward to his visits whenever he would stop and chat with me. Because he was so warm and outgoing, it was hard to be shy around him. He was the type of person who naturally drew you out of your shell.

"Hi! How are you?"

"Happy to be here," he replied. "What about you? Still living on the sunny side of life?"

I grinned at him. "Today's been amazing,

actually."

He said in mock arrogance, "I'm here, so of course it is. Besides me, what made it so good?"

"Rhys returned from Italy and brought me back the most incredible gifts." I wanted to pinch myself in disbelief they were mine. "Look."

I opened the box to show him. Jules leaned against my counter and whistled when he saw my bow ties. "Wow, Zapfirino? How fancy."

"Rhys is too generous. I still can't believe he gave them to me."

"I'm happy for you! My brother likes Zapfirino's stuff."

"I didn't know you had a brother," I commented in surprise.

He nodded. "Yeah, he's a few years younger than me. His name is Rooney, but he goes by Rune."

"What a cool nickname."

"You'd probably get along with him really well, now that I'm thinking about it," Jules said. "He's quieter and his humor is pretty dry, but he's more open once he gets to know you. It just takes a bit of effort to break through his prickly hedgehog quills first."

I laughed at the description. "That sounds refreshing, actually. Everyone I know here is so lively and outgoing. I'm usually much more on the shy and reserved side myself."

"A quiet chat over coffee is what my brother

needs. He tends to be a lone-wolf type, so it would be nice for him to have a wonderful friend like you. Does tomorrow work for you?"

Back in Dublin, Gregory had been one of my only friends. The old me would have been too scared to meet a stranger. But after becoming a part of Felix's group, I had learned that marvelous things happened when I opened myself up to letting people into my life. Meeting someone to be their friend was so much less pressure than a date. After all, I already knew how to be a friend.

I had sort of inherited Felix and his friends through Augie. They treated me like one of their best mates they had known for years, but having a friend of my own was appealing. It sounded like Rune was someone I could relax and be my normal self around without everything being so boisterous all the time. He may not be as outgoing as Jules, but I bet he was equally kind.

"If he's interested, I think I'd enjoy that." A nervous thrill ran through me at accepting the offer.

"In that case, I'll ask him about it tonight and set something up for you. I can send you the details afterward. Sound good?"

"Yes, thank you." I wrote my mobile number on memo paper so he could message me later.

Xander walked over and gave his best friend a playfully suspicious look. "Oh, god, now what are you planning?"

He put the paper in his pocket with a grin. "I want to introduce Callum to Rune. They'd be great for each other, don't you think?"

He tilted his head as he considered it. "Huh, that's actually not a terrible idea."

"It's a fantastic idea, thank you very much." I loved watching the two of them banter. Sometimes I wondered if there was more between them than friendship, but it wasn't my place to speculate.

"Only if you can get him to agree to it," Xander countered.

"I've gotten quite good at hedgehog wrangling over the years. He'll agree."

Xander scoffed. "Probably only to prove you wrong."

"That's fine with me. The important thing is that he goes," Jules said with a shrug.

"Your brother could use some sunshine in his life."

I blushed when Jules replied, "That's why Callum is perfect for the cute little rain cloud I call a brother."

"You know Rune would absolutely hate you for calling him that, right?"

"Of course! That's why I do it. The best part of being an older brother is annoying the hell out of your cute baby brother."

"Somewhere, Rune is rolling his eyes at you for that comment." Xander shook his head with a sigh. "Ready to go?"

"As soon as you are."

"Let's head out, then." Xander told me, "I'll be back at one for you to take lunch, okay?"

"Sure, that sounds great."

Before they walked away, Jules promised, "I'll text you later tonight about when and where to meet my brother tomorrow."

"Thanks!"

I watched as they left together and wondered if maybe Rune and I could have that kind of relationship someday. It would be wonderful to be close like Jules and Xander were. I missed that bond where you could tell that one person in your life everything. Although, even with Gregory, there had constantly been a wall between us that I hid my sexuality behind because I had been so afraid of losing him. Learning I was right to fear him was a minor consolation in the ugly reality of what happened. At least I didn't have any lingering feelings for him to get me down.

That was all old history and no longer mattered. I focused on the excitement over meeting Rune. We hadn't even met yet, but we already shared an appreciation for Gio Zapfirino. If nothing else, I could talk to him about that. The thought of bonding with someone over that made me smile at the box of bow ties still sitting on my desk. It was silly, but I sort of felt like they had brought me good luck by helping introduce me to Rune.

Rather than daydreaming about what meeting him would be like, I returned to my work instead.

Chapter Two

RUNE

I KNEW my life had reached a new low when fucking made me feel worse instead of better. It apparently didn't matter that I had money, fame, and a hot guy in bed with me who was willing to do anything I asked. I still felt hollow, with no idea how to fill that aching void inside me. It begged for something to make it stop, but I couldn't figure out what it yearned for so desperately. Sex had always fixed things, even if it was only for a little while. Now, even that didn't work anymore. *Goddamn it.*

The weight of my anxiety sat heavily on my chest, making it difficult to breathe. That meant it was time to escape from my latest hookup and return to the sanctuary of my apartment. Not wanting to wake up—shit, I didn't even remember his name. Dawson? Darius? Dane, maybe? Fuck it, it's not like it mattered. I'd never see the guy again.

Whatever his name was, I didn't want to wake him up and risk having an awkward conversation. I slipped out of bed, eager to get the hell out of there before he noticed. Stealthily getting dressed, I thought I was in the clear until I heard his groggy voice ask, "Where are you going, Rune?"

"Home." I pulled out my phone to arrange for a car to pick me up so I could escape. Damn my car for being in the shop for service. I loved vintage Ferraris, but they were a pain in the ass to upkeep.

What's-his-name rolled onto his side, the sheets dipping low on his hips. He was undeniably attractive, but he wasn't enough to save me from my apathy. I wasn't sure what could.

"Why don't you come back to bed instead?"

"I've got work." It was a lie, but he didn't know that.

"It's still early. The sun's barely out yet."

Rather than giving in, I put on my red leather jacket, then did my cursory check to make sure I had my wallet, phone, and keys on me. The last thing I wanted was a reason to come back. My lies continued to pile up. "See you around."

"You really won't stay?" He pouted, drawing my attention to his full lips that had sucked my cock so masterfully hours earlier. Why wasn't that enough anymore?

Ignoring his protests, I didn't bother apologizing as I left. Once outside, I turned my collar up against the chill in the early morning air. The gray dawn drained the color from everything, which was appropriate on such a miserable day. How long had it been since my life had been vibrant? It was such a distant memory that it had faded into sepia, leaving me alone in a black-and-white world I didn't belong in anymore. *Shit, now I'm getting maudlin.*

My car pulled up, temporarily saving me from my morose thoughts. The reprieve lasted only as long as it took to get into the back seat. My mood returned heavier than before as I watched the streets fly by in a monochromatic blur. I told myself a shower and some sleep would improve my outlook, but even I couldn't believe that lie.

HOURS LATER, I still didn't feel any better. On the upside, I didn't feel worse. I didn't feel anything, other than that ever-present ache that pleaded for something to matter to me again. It shouldn't be so difficult to be happy, especially when I had every luxury money could buy and any man I desired thanks to my successful career and good looks. But none of it brought me any joy or peace. It all felt so meaningless that it was hard not to despair. What kind of sick joke was it that I had everything and nothing at the same time?

I looked out the window at the dreary afternoon

with a heavy sigh. A bleak rain fell, almost like the sky was crying tears I no longer knew how to shed. It was a minor consolation. If it was a beautiful sunny day, that would only make a mockery out of my misery.

A knock on the door drew me from my moody musings. I walked over and saw through the peephole it was my older brother, Jules. He meant well, but I wasn't up to his relentless optimism. It was easier to pretend I wasn't home—at least until he called out, "I know you're in there, Rune. Let me in."

I reacted on autopilot as I opened the door. He greeted me with a bright smile and a tight hug. God, I *loathed* hugging, but my brother was like a determined boa constrictor who wanted to squeeze the fluff out of you. I loved him enough to put up with it, but on such a bleak day, it made it harder to tolerate.

His voice was warm as he asked, "How're you doing?"

"No worse than usual." I led him into my living room. Professionally decorated in an impersonal black and chrome, it looked more like a staged home in a lifestyle magazine than somewhere someone lived. Like everything else in my life, it was all for show. My office was the only place in the entire apartment that reflected who I really was. It was my sole sanctuary, where no one was allowed to go. The only person besides me who had ever entered it was Jules once when he was helping me move in a few years ago.

After we sat down, he looked at me with so much

concern that guilt churned in my gut. "I'm worried about you."

I couldn't blame him. I'd be worried about me too if I could muster up the energy to give a fuck. It was so bad that I couldn't even find it within myself to placate him. "Worrying doesn't change anything."

"I know what will help."

He said it with such confidence, but I knew better. I had tried everything I could think of, but nothing worked. "You can save your breath. I'm already in therapy."

He laughed at my response, but I didn't have it in me to join in.

"What you need is a friend."

I rolled my eyes at his suggestion. "I have friends, thanks."

"No, other than Maria and Renée, you have a lot of acquaintances you barely tolerate and men you fuck," he argued. "I'm talking about an *actual* friend. Someone you can be your true self with, who is there for you no matter what and not because of who you are."

"And where am I supposed to find this magical friend that doesn't know or care that I'm Rune Tourneau, the world-famous model?"

My brother always had an answer for everything. "His name is Callum, and he works for Xander. I want you to meet him."

"Are you seriously trying to set me up on a

playdate? For fuck's sake, Jules, I'm thirty! I'm way too old for that shit."

"Yeah, because you're doing *so* well on your own in that department."

"All I need is a warm body and a good fuck." The bitter cynicism of my declaration left an acrid taste in my mouth. The worst part was yesterday had proven that wasn't even true anymore.

He shook his head with a disappointed expression that pained me. "No, what you need to do is let someone into your heart who cares about you and stop wallowing in your pity party of one."

I ignored the jab. "And what makes you think this Callum guy is that person?"

"He's a good kid with a kind—"

"*Kid?*"

He quickly backpedaled. "Sorry, he's not a *kid*-kid. That was a poor choice of words. He's only a kid to me because I'm thirty-three."

"How old is he?"

Jules at least had the decency to look sheepish. "Almost twenty-one, but—"

"He's not even old enough to legally drink!"

My brother refused to relent. "He is in Ireland."

"What the fuck does the drinking age in Ireland have to do with anything?"

"That's where he's from," Jules explained. "He moved here a few months ago and could really use a friend. And since you also need one, it's a great idea."

I started ticking off points on my fingers. "One, I won't have anything in common with a twenty-year-old kid. Two, I don't *need* a friend, let alone one whose idea of communicating is sending stupid memes. Three—"

He interrupted me to address my concerns. "Look, he's mature for his age. And you *do* need a friend. Do you not understand you're lonely?"

"How can I be lonely when I have a different man in bed any night I want?"

"If that's true, then why does it make you feel so empty afterward?" That silenced my next objection, because he was right, even though I hadn't confided in him about it. "It's unsatisfying because you're yearning for a connection with someone that's about more than getting off. Take it from me—hanging out with Xander is better than any meaningless fuck, no matter how hot the guy is."

Given how deep in denial Jules was about his feelings for Xander, he wasn't in any position to be giving me advice in that area. "Is that what you tell yourself to sleep at night?"

"Hey, don't get nasty because you're pissed I'm right," he shot back. "Whether or not you want to admit it, you're missing out by not having someone special in your life. You just don't know it because you've always been a lone wolf."

"And your solution is offering me an innocent sheep?"

"All I'm asking is that you meet Callum for coffee with an open mind," he said. "He doesn't know who you are."

"I find that hard to believe. You'd have to live under a rock or been in a coma to not have seen that damn cologne commercial I did." It had made me a fortune but had proven to be the bane of my existence. Mercifully, in the intervening years, I no longer got harassed about it on a daily basis when I was out in public.

"Fair enough," he conceded. "But even if he makes that connection, he won't treat you any differently. Callum's not like that. He's a genuinely good guy, Rune. Trust me, you need that kind of person in your life."

Ever since I had catapulted to fame years ago, only my family and Xander treated me like I was normal. Someone treating me like a regular person was almost a foreign concept after years of dealing with fawning fans. Most people only cared about Rune the Mannequin, who used his pretty face and sex to sell overpriced luxuries to people with more money than sense.

But I had to admit, it would be nice to just be me for once without having to worry about someone's ulterior motives for getting close to me. Maybe Jules was right, and I *was* lonely. Other than him, I didn't have anyone I could reach out to on a shitty day to make me feel better. And my life had been full of those kinds of days lately.

My brother never did this kind of thing, so if he was asking, it was because he really believed that it would be best for me. As much as he had done for me over the years, I at least owed it to him to meet this guy once. "Fine, I'll meet him, but only under one condition. You won't complain or ask me to go out with him again after he acts like every other person who's ever met me."

"It's a deal." He pulled out his phone and texted me the details. "I told Callum you would find him at the Brewhaha Café, so he can't look you up beforehand. He's cute, wears bow ties, has red hair, and gorgeous dark blue eyes. You can't miss him."

I copied the info into my calendar before putting my phone away. The meeting with Callum would probably end up being a waste of time, but it wasn't like I had anything else to do tomorrow. I knew better than to expect anything other than the worst-case scenario, but for the first time in years, embers of hope stirred in my heart. It would be nice if he was what I had unknowingly been searching for all along.

Chapter Three

CALLUM

IT WAS difficult to calm myself as I waited at the Brewhaha Café for Rune to appear. Even though it was a meeting with a potential new friend and not a date, my nerves frayed from doing something so far out of my comfort zone.

I was totally overdressed for the occasion, but it comforted me. Jeans and a hoodie weren't my style, so I chose a dark blue suit, paired with a teal shirt and my new floral paisley Zapfirino bow tie. It made me feel better, plus I hoped it would make me look a little older.

Part of my nervousness was from Jules telling me that his younger brother would find me at the café. I had no idea what Rune looked like, realizing too late that I didn't know their last name to try looking him up beforehand. I could have asked Xander, but I refused to bother him with such a silly question about a personal matter. That meant I had no choice but to wait for Rune to come over to me. The small sitting area was almost empty, so he shouldn't miss me. But I fretted about it anyway because that was how my shite brain worked.

I sipped my amazing hot cocoa, savoring the flavor. A lot of places used bitter chocolates, but this one was the perfect amount of sweet. I set the ceramic mug back on the table as my gaze once again travelled around the room in search of the mysterious Rune. Would we even have anything in common beyond excellent taste in a fashion designer?

Jules seemed to think we would become close, so I hoped he was right. As much as I loved hanging out with Augie's brother, Felix, and his group of friends, I wanted my own friend.

Sunlight flooded into the café when the front door opened, drawing my attention. My breathing hitched at the sight of the magnificent man who walked in. He was the very definition of tall, dark, and handsome. Dressed in a black three-piece suit, cobalt-colored shirt, and pastel blue tie, he was a god amongst men. His black hair was the right amount of mussed to be stylish without being a mess. With his sharp cheekbones and strong jaw, he was the sexiest and most beautiful person I had ever seen. Even his eyebrows were bloody perfect.

It was rude to gawk, but I couldn't look away. I stiffened when he glanced in my direction, and our gazes met. An electric jolt ricocheted through me as I stared into his arctic-blue eyes. That powerful connection between us made my heart race as my mind blanked of every thought other than *fuckfuckfuckfuckfuckingfuck!*

The corner of his mouth turned upward in a slight smirk, sending the butterflies inside me into a tizzy. When he finally broke eye contact to move up in the line for the cashier, I gasped for air. Wow, I hadn't realized I had literally quit breathing because he was breathtakingly stunning.

I placed my hand over my heart, stunned by how fast it was racing from that single glance in my direction. Never in my life had I been so physically affected by someone before. But that was no ordinary man. No, he was walking sex who tempted you with lustful thoughts of sinning in unforgivable ways.

Despite being caught staring, my gaze kept darting over to him as he placed his order. I couldn't blame the barista helping him for being flustered. He was too much sexy to handle at such a close proximity. Even with half the café between us and not a single word exchanged, I barely survived without humiliating myself.

I forced myself to focus on my drink, resisting the siren call to look at him again. He probably hated being ogled at by everyone in awe of his beauty. I didn't want him to assume I was a creep, so I respectfully averted my gaze, while dying for one more glimpse before he left the café.

My good intentions went out the window when he walked over to my table with a mug. Without meaning to, I looked up from his impossibly long legs, to his lean torso and broad shoulders, and to his flawless face.

I attempted to apologize for my rudeness, but I couldn't make a sound as I got lost in the ocean of his eyes. They were an icy blue, but full of a fire that beckoned for me to come closer. The intense connection from before returned in a rush, making it harder to breathe. How was it possible that even his long eyelashes were captivating?

"You must be Callum."

The deep timbre of his voice saying my name made heat pool in my belly, while it raised chills on my skin. Too stunned to reply, I nodded in response.

He held out his free hand. "I'm Rune. Nice to meet you."

My reflexes reacted before my brain did, so I reached out to him. The instant our palms touched, my arousal sparked into a roaring blaze that made me inhale in surprise. In doing so, I smelled his cologne. It was dark and inviting, spiced with a hint of something unknown that had me biting my lower lip to hold in a moan. *Fuck me.*

It became even more difficult to restrain myself when his long, slender fingers wrapped around me as we shook hands. His touch was electric, making every nerve inside me come to life. An image flashed in my mind of him caressing my naked body, shocking me with the graphic thought of us entwined in a sensual embrace as we fucked. The fires of desire raged in me like never before, scaring me with how intensely I experienced the pull of instant attraction to him.

My voice sounded as if it belonged to somebody else as I replied, "The pleasure's mine."

His knowing smirk caused my heart to stutter in my chest as I struggled against my hormones that had never gone so haywire over someone before. I mourned the loss of contact when he pulled away to sit down across from me. The experience disoriented me. *What the hell just happened?*

Emboldened by my lust, my first response had been full of a confident innuendo that was completely foreign to me. With the slight distance between us, I was back to stumbling over what to say next. "Um, hi? Hello. Hi."

His amused smile at my sudden turn into awkwardness melted me into a quivering puddle. "Hi."

The single-syllable word sent shivers racing down my spine. What was it about this man that every little thing he did was sexual? Especially how he slid his fingers through the hole of his mug grip, giving me ideas I wasn't equipped to handle. *Christ Almighty, save me from myself. I'm not going to make it.*

He was so perfect I almost couldn't believe he was real. Yet, I had to find the wherewithal to have a proper conversation with him. I could barely remember my own name with him watching me, let alone how to talk to someone as hot as him. No wonder Jules didn't want me to know what his brother looked like beforehand. Rune was so attractive I would have been too intimidated to meet him.

I wanted to pick up my cocoa, but my trembling fingers would betray how physically affected I was by his presence. Instead, I relied on the respectful manners Ma taught me. "Thank you for meeting me today."

"My brother never makes requests, so it piqued my curiosity."

Not wanting him to have the wrong impression, I defended myself. "Jules suggested this to me. I'm somewhat new to the area, so he thought it would be an excellent idea for us to meet. I didn't ask him."

"If you had, I never would have agreed."

The statement confused me. "How could I have asked when I didn't know you existed until yesterday?"

He seemed entertained by my answer, but I couldn't understand why. "You don't know our last name, do you?"

"No, Xander introduced him as just Jules the first time I met him. It never occurred to me to ask since it didn't seem relevant."

He grinned in delight at my response. His expression made me feel flushed. I could only pray my cheeks weren't as pink as they felt. "What do you know about me?"

The situation was bewildering enough to make it easier to talk. "You're Jules's younger brother. Rooney is your actual name, but you go by Rune. You also like the designer Gio Zapfirino. Jules said we might get along and be friends, so we should meet. He told me you would find me here at the café."

"That's it?"

I replied before thinking it through. "Um, he may have also referred to you as a hedgehog and a cute little rain cloud."

"Of course he did." Rune rolled his eyes before taking a long sip of his coffee. "Interesting."

"What is?" He lost me, and not just because he was so damn attractive that I almost forgot the English language.

"You genuinely have no clue who I am."

I couldn't tell if I was passing or failing a test I didn't even realize I was taking until it was too late. "Sorry, I don't—"

"No, please don't be sorry. It's a good thing. Incredible, actually."

Baffled, I tilted my head as I studied him. "Why?"

Rune leaned forward and gazed deep into my soul. I once again forgot what air was, his scent stoking the ashes inside of me back into a burning flame. His blue eyes were hypnotic in their power over me. I got so tied up in him I almost missed him asking, "I really don't seem the least bit familiar to you?"

Entranced by him, my stupid gob spoke before I could stop myself. "No, I'd never forget someone as gorgeous as you."

While I felt like an idiot for saying it out loud, it was true. I used to have a crush on my brother's friend, Donnelly, who was handsome and had become a famous model in Ireland. But even he couldn't hold a candle to the sexy man sitting across from me, setting my soul alight with an unfamiliar passionate need.

His chuckle made me shudder as the rich sound of it washed over me. I didn't understand my own visceral reactions to him, but they were powerful and primal. "My brother's right. We'll get along great."

"Because I don't know who you are?" What sense did that make?

"Partially."

The conversation kept tripping me up. "What's the other reason?"

"If we become good enough friends, I'll answer you then." It would have been annoying how enigmatic he was if it didn't further enhance his alluring mystique. "Tell me about yourself."

My life suddenly seemed very boring sitting near

someone so remarkable. "There's not much to say, really."

"Everyone has a story."

It took an effort to act normal and do as he requested. "I'm from Dublin but moved here about five months ago to live with my older brother and his boyfriend. They're friends with Rhys, so I work at his company as Xander's assistant. Jules comes to the office sometimes to meet up with Xander for lunch, so that's how I met him."

"Rhys must pay you well if you can afford Gio Zapfirino bow ties as an assistant."

I touched the one I was wearing, still in awe of the fact Rhys had given me such an incredible present. "He's one of the most generous people I've ever met, but my salary isn't quite *that* good. This was a gift from him. He came back from Italy this week and gave me three of them as a thank-you for all the hard work I've done. I collect bow ties, so it was thoughtful of him."

He looked impressed, which made me feel chuffed with pleasure. "Damn, that's one hell of a nice boss."

"Yeah, he's the best," I insisted. "If it weren't for him, I would have had to go back to Ireland. I'm grateful he allows me to work for him and Xander so I can stay here with my brother."

"Jules has always spoken highly of Rhys. He must be great if Xander is willing to be dedicated to him.

You must be an exceptional employee to get that kind of present after being there only a few months."

The praise launched the butterflies into flight inside me again as I blushed. "I try to make myself useful. It's the least I can do to thank him for helping me out when I needed it the most."

"I take it things were tough back in Ireland?"

"You could say that." I touched the side of my face where Gregory had given me a shiner. The bruise had healed months ago, but the pain lingered on my soul sometimes. "I'm much better off here. This is the happiest I've ever been, honestly. I love living in Sunnyside with Brody and Augie. Life is much more fun now."

"I'm glad you found a place to belong. That's important."

"It is," I agreed. "I'm using this opportunity to be a better version of me. I've challenged myself to say yes to things that scare me."

"Like jumping out of a plane?"

I laughed. "No, absolutely not. There's nothing in the world that would get me to agree to that. I'm trying to be brave, not stupid."

"Ah, so you mean taking a chance on meeting a stranger to make a new friend?"

"Yeah." It sounded embarrassingly simple when he put it that way, but it was an enormous step for me. "I've always been quiet and awkward, so it's hard to put myself out there. That probably sounds stupid to you, but—"

"No, not at all. Being an introvert in an extrovert world is difficult. I get that, trust me."

Relief flooded through me that he understood and didn't think I was being a baby about it. "Exactly! But I've learned that coming out of my shell a little has made a huge difference in my life. Six months ago, I wouldn't have been able to come here today."

"Well, I'm glad you did." He lifted his mug in a small toast.

It was too unbelievable to wrap my head around. "You are?"

"Sincerely."

How was that possible? "But all I've done is embarrass myself."

"No, you've authentically been yourself. To me, that's remarkable and worth coming here today to meet you."

"Why?"

"Because the world is filled with people who will say and do anything to get what they want out of you." His cynicism came through loud and clear. "I'm surrounded by sycophants who tell me what they think I want to hear instead of telling me the truth. Your honesty is refreshing."

"That sounds tough."

He smiled at me with a warmth that felt like a comforting embrace. I wished I could wrap myself up in that sensation and stay there forever. "I forgot people like you existed. I've never been more glad to have been proven wrong."

The sentiment was touching, but I still didn't understand. "People like me? What do you mean?"

"A good person who sees me for who I really am, instead of who they want me to be. Other than my family and Xander, I've never had anyone else I could say that about until I met you."

It sounded so lonely to me. In that moment, I understood Jules hadn't only been trying to find me a new friend—he had done it for his brother's sake, too. It made it easier to tell him, "I don't know why anyone would want you to be different, when you're already incredible."

"Thank you, Callum."

Hearing him say my name once again brought chills to my skin as his voice caressed it intimately. It felt like he was thanking me for even more than I realized, despite my bumbling fumbles. "You're welcome."

Realizing that somebody as stunning as Rune could be so lonely came as quite a shock. However, I could see how easily someone could put him on a high, untouchable pedestal. I resolved myself to never do that to him. He deserved to have a good friend, and I hoped I could be that for him. I'd have to learn how to ignore my body's intimate responses to him. It was a small price to pay, though.

Of course, part of being someone's friend was knowing them well. It felt awkward to ask, but I forged ahead. "So, what should I know about you?"

He thought about it for a moment. "I love to cook, which surprises people. Everyone assumes I live on kale protein shakes and salads, which couldn't be further from the truth."

An image of him wearing one of those silly *Kiss the cook* aprons came to mind, giving me thoughts I shouldn't have. I refocused myself. "What do you like to make?"

"Mostly Italian and French food, but I'm good with a grill. I also enjoy making desserts."

Why did *everything* about him have to be perfect? "That's so impressive! Desserts are my favorite."

He grinned at my amazement. "Based on your response, I'm guessing you don't cook much?"

There was no trace of judgment in his tone, but I still flushed in embarrassment. "I can do enough to get by, but Augie prefers to make dinner for us. I help him with prep, so I'm not completely useless. I did the same thing for Ma back home."

"A cook always benefits from having a talented sous chef." I appreciated his effort to reassure me about my lack of skills. "What do you enjoy doing?"

"I read a lot of history books and autobiographies. Sometimes I'll read fantasy, too. I'll pick up anything that seems interesting, or that someone recommends me."

"History's my favorite, too." My heart skipped a beat with excitement at discovering a shared passion. "Even studying it in college didn't stop me from loving it, which is saying something."

"The British monarchy and Russian empire fascinate me the most, but I've never been able to study them beyond my own reading." I tried not to feel a pang of regret about not having the chance to do that now. Without Da's support, it wasn't financially possible anymore for me to go to university. "What's your favorite area?"

I wasn't expecting him to say, "I got my master's degree in the French Revolution."

How was it fair that he was so gorgeous *and* smart? I was in complete awe of him. "Does that mean you're also fluent in French?"

"I lived in Paris and Milan for a few years, so I learned French and Italian."

The thought of him speaking those languages sent a shudder of pleasure through me. Realizing I was getting off-track, I looped back around to the main point. "Can I ask why you specialized in the French Revolution?"

He seemed surprised by my question. "You really want to know?"

"Please, I would love to hear more about it."

Rune silently regarded me for a long moment, as if he were trying to figure out some grand mystery. I almost thought he wouldn't tell me when he began speaking. "It's a fascinating mess of contradictions."

"How so?"

"The revolution was a movement based on the high ideals of the Enlightenment period. But it also led to one of the most brutal eras of history with the Reign of Terror," he explained. "Their admirable motto of *liberty, equality, fraternity* was fundamentally at odds with the reality of the Republic they were building. The dark irony of it all intrigues me."

"What do you mean it was at odds?"

He answered my question with one of his own. "What does the word 'equality' mean to you regarding people?"

"That everyone is equal, regardless of their gender, race, sexual orientation, age, or financial circumstance." I worried it was too simplistic an answer. "All people are the same no matter what."

"Right, that's what it *should* mean," he agreed. "However, in the *Declaration of the Rights of Man and of the Citizen*, equality only applied to male property owners over the age of twenty-five. That meant only a little over four million people out of twenty-nine million, since women, slaves, children, and foreigners were excluded. Not very equal, is it?"

"No, not at all," I said with a frown.

"There were many women writers who protested and fought for inclusion, like Olympe de Gouges. And they paid with their lives to do it. That's why I focused my thesis on exploring the voices silenced by the unequal equality during the Revolution."

His topic sounded so interesting that I wanted to read it, but I didn't feel right requesting permission. Instead, I settled for asking, "Who was she?"

"There's no need to be polite. I won't get offended if you're not interested."

How could he think it bored me to learn about something so fascinating? "No, I'm genuinely curious."

Rune hesitated, almost like he was afraid to believe me. It amazed me that someone as perfect as him could ever have a moment of uncertainty. He drank his coffee before answering. "She was an incredible woman who wrote a rebuttal called *Declaration of the Rights of Woman and the Female Citizen*. In it, she demanded that the women who fought as part of the Revolution be given true equality to stand on the same level with men."

"Wow, that must have been so dangerous back then."

"It was," he agreed. "Because Olympe didn't stop there. She also was staunchly against slavery in the French colonies and argued for human rights, which earned her a lot of enemies. In the end, they guillotined her for being so defiantly vocal about her beliefs."

"How have I never heard of her before? She sounds fascinating."

He ruefully shook his head. "Because asshole men were in charge of writing history. They were fond of burying strong women like her who questioned the status quo by discrediting their achievements. It's total bullshit."

"There must be so many more stories like hers out there that we never get to hear because of that."

"More than we can even fathom." He finished his coffee, then set it on the table. "That's why the imagery of the French Revolution always confused me."

"The imagery?"

Now that he wasn't holding his mug, Rune became more animated with his hands while talking. It was beautiful to watch. "Yes, because the ideals of liberty, equality, fraternity, and reason were personified in the symbol of an idealized woman. Yet, real women weren't being treated fairly under the new doctrines that Lady Liberty represented."

I tried to puzzle through the situation. "That doesn't make any sense, though. Why would they use a woman for a symbol when they didn't have the same rights that the art represents?"

"There's a lot of speculation, but not one straightforward answer."

"That's too bad." I would have loved to know the reason behind the logic.

"I can't imagine how frustrating it must have been to see a female icon heralding a new value system that didn't actually apply to you. The insurmountable gap between the ideological female representation of the Republic's civic virtues and the actuality of women's unequal status during that period must have been maddening."

His enthusiasm for the subject made it so much easier to relate to him. I could hardly believe he geeked out over history like I did. It made me wish I knew more than a few basic facts about the French Revolution. "You mentioned earlier that Olympe was guillotined for speaking out. I think I heard that they invented the guillotine to make executions better for the victims, but maybe I'm misremembering. Then again, there isn't a humane method to kill somebody, so…"

"Compared to how they used to execute people, the guillotine actually was *way* more humane." Damn, talk about a depressing thought. "That's another one of those fascinating twisted ironies. They developed the guillotine in accordance with the values of the Enlightenment so that capital punishment was no longer savage. Yet, they utilized it to slaughter almost seventeen thousand people during the Reign of Terror."

The death toll shocked me, despite a vague knowledge about that period of history being grim. "How long was the Reign of Terror?"

"Specific dates are another thing that historians disagree on. Some argue it was in 1792 or 1793, while others think it started in July 1789 with the first death of the revolution. Regardless, it ended in July 1794 when Maximilien Robespierre fell from power and was executed by the very guillotine he had championed."

"That's…" I trailed off because I couldn't put into words my feelings on the matter. It was so many people in such a short amount of time it was hard to fathom.

For the first time since meeting Rune, he seemed embarrassed. A neutral mask of indifference replaced his open expressiveness while talking about his passion. It once again made him seem untouchable and gave me an unfamiliar urge to tear down every brick out of that wall he had thrown up between us. I wanted to reach him before he could lock himself away again.

He ruffled his dark hair, which did funny things to my heart. "Sorry, I didn't mean to get so heavy. That's far more information than you needed. I appreciate you indulging my inner academic nerd. It rarely gets to come out and play, so I got a little overzealous."

"No, please don't apologize." I felt guilty for making him self-conscious, even as I marveled that someone like him could feel that way. "That was such a large number in a brief time span, I wasn't sure what to say. But hearing all of this was fascinating! I regret not reading about the French Revolution before."

He looked a little dubious, almost like he didn't believe me. "You weren't bored?"

"How could anyone be bored hearing that? I would sign up and take a class with you about this if I could."

"You don't have to say that to be nice, you know."

His words from earlier about people always telling him what he wanted to hear came back to me. I realized how hard it must be for him to trust somebody. It gave me the strength to be bolder than I normally would have been. "I promise I'm not saying it only to humor you. Your research is fascinating, and I want to learn more about it because of you. I think you're amazing!"

He arched an eyebrow skeptically as his voice took on a hard edge. "Because guys who look like me aren't supposed to be smart?"

The implication horrified me. "No, it's because you care about the voices of people who weren't listened to. It genuinely moved me, plus it's obvious how passionate you are about this. That's what's so wonderful to me. I'm sorry you thought I was judging you. I sincerely enjoyed hearing you talk about your research."

His expression softened into a gentle smile I tried very hard not to swoon over. "It seems I owe you another apology."

"Not at all. You don't owe me any."

"I grew so accustomed to everyone's eyes glazing

over whenever I brought up history that I never discuss it anymore. There's no point when so many people hate it," Rune said, once again making my heart go out to him. "But it wasn't fair of me to judge you based on other people's reactions when you were being sincere. Thanks for allowing me to share that with you."

The glimpse into his loneliness made me ache for him. "Please talk to me about history whenever you want. It's a subject I've always enjoyed. I can show you on my phone how many history e-books I have if you don't believe me. Or, we can take a deep dive into the Plantagenets and the War of the Roses so I can show you how easily I can geek out over this kind of stuff, too."

He chuckled, the sound relieving the tension I felt over accidentally offending him. I loved how his laughter made the light dance in his beautiful eyes. "No, I believe you. The fact that you even know the word 'Plantagenets' is solid proof. That's a conversation we should have another day."

My hopes swelled that he wanted to see me again. "You want to meet up again?"

"I'd be a shitty friend if I didn't. Speaking of which, I should give you my number."

I couldn't stop myself from beaming with happiness as we exchanged our information. Considering how otherworldly Rune's level of beauty was, I never expected to have so much in common with him. It was an excellent reminder of why you shouldn't judge anyone before getting to know them. Maybe it was pathetic to be so excited about making a new friend. That didn't stop me from feeling blessed to have seen the real side of him I suspected few people were allowed to see.

Chapter Four

RUNE

"IN ANOTHER LIFE, you would have been an incredible chef," Jules praised me after finishing the grilled chicken breast with pea and mushroom risotto I'd prepared for us to enjoy. Next to him in jeans with a lavender polo shirt, I was overdressed in my gray suit and purple tartan tie.

"Sure, minus the whole high-stress situation of leading a team of people through a hectic service aspect of running a kitchen."

"With your good looks, you could easily be a reality TV chef. You should talk to your agent about it."

"You need to be famous for cooking, and not just a well-known pretty face," I pointed out. "Besides, my sarcastic personality isn't exactly made for TV."

"Tell that to Gordon Ramsay." He continued trying to sell me on his idea. "It's worth thinking about down the road if you ever leave the modeling industry."

I'd much rather go back to grad school and get my PhD in history, but I didn't say that to my brother. Instead, I cleared the dishes and cleaned up the kitchen as he attempted to persuade me about his alternative life plan for me while he helped.

After we finished and settled in my living room, Jules requested, "Spill it."

I feigned ignorance. "Spill what? The metaphorical tea?"

"Tell me how it went with Callum."

"It was fine." That was a bit of an understatement. Callum had turned out to be a pleasant surprise. It had been three days since I met him in the café, but I couldn't get him off my mind. He unintentionally stirred up things inside me which had lain dormant for far too long.

Jules gave me a knowing look. "It had to at least go well enough that you didn't complain to me about being forced into meeting him. So, what did you think?"

"He's…" I struggled to put into words what I thought of Callum. He had been so warm and genuine, not to mention precious in his enthusiasm. It had been a refreshing experience that I still wasn't certain what to make of it. "He's kind."

Jules arched his eyebrows at me. "He's *kind*? That's all you have to say about him?"

"You were right about him having no idea who I am." That much had been apparent to me when I noticed Callum's almost comically wide-eyed reaction to my entrance into the café. He had stared at me in awe but lacked the spark of recognition and accompanying excitement about meeting someone famous most people had when they saw me. When we shook hands, I hadn't been able to hold back my smirk at the unintentional whimper that had escaped him. It had been endearing to watch him being so flustered while trying hard to act normal in front of me. It was oddly touching he made that kind of effort for me. "I tried to bait him into asking who I was, but he let me keep my secrets."

"That's because even if he knew, it wouldn't change anything for him."

Jules had asserted the same claim when attempting to entice me into meet Callum, but now I knew it was true. "He differed from what I imagined."

"Meaning you could have an actual conversation with him?"

"Yeah." It amazed me I had accidentally exposed a part of myself to Callum I kept hidden from everyone else. But when he had brought up a shared interest in history and asked questions about my research, I lost myself to my excitement. It had been so long since I had indulged in talking about history, I embarrassed myself by going overboard with grim details of the Reign of Terror. My residual humiliation over doing that lingered.

Days later, I also still felt like an asshole for accusing him of assuming someone who looked like me couldn't be smart. I experienced an unfamiliar pang of regret for my callous behavior over causing him to be distressed about upsetting me. He had been sincere with his interest, and I repaid it by presuming the worst of him. Him being so gracious about my blunder and hurrying to reassure me told me a lot about him.

My conversation with Callum reminded me of how much I missed history. It had been almost five years since I graduated from my master's program, but there was no practical use for my degree in the modeling world. They needed you to be gorgeous, not intelligent. I yearned for that three-year period of my life where I had been surrounded by like-minded academics. It made me nostalgic for my days of teaching, back when I enjoyed sharing my knowledge and joy with undergrads who were just starting their academic careers.

"Maybe now you understand why I thought the two of you needed each other," Jules said, pulling me from my musings.

I started to protest I didn't need anyone, but I caught myself. Meeting Callum had been the only bright spot in recent memory. It was the first time in god knows how long I had almost felt like myself instead of just an empty shell housing other people's expectations.

Jules remained patient with me. "Do you want to see him again?"

The answer to his question was a resounding yes, but it wasn't that easy. I longed to talk with Callum again, but the very fact that I wanted to kept me from reaching out to him. Our one meeting had gone well, but my inner pessimist was convinced the next time would be a crushing disappointment. Yet, there was a tiny voice inside of me whispering with the utmost certainty it would be different with him. I had no reason to trust the kid, so why did part of me desperately want to? Why did I want him to prove me wrong and be the sincere person he represented himself as?

My turmoil must have shown in my expression, because Jules's gaze softened as he looked at me. "It's okay that you wish you could spend more time with him, Rune. It would be good for both of you."

"I doubt it. He hasn't texted me asking me to meet up with him again."

Jules bit his lower lip to keep back his laughter at my petulant response. "Come on, be reasonable. You know damn well he was so overwhelmed by you he doesn't feel like he's allowed to text you first. His ego is nonexistent. If anything, he's probably beating himself up over embarrassing himself so badly you never want to talk to him again."

The idea that Callum would be self-flagellating in

regret over our time together turned my stomach. After three days of no contact, I could only imagine what awful stories he had told himself to believe. It made sense that's how someone like him would react. I hated feeling responsible for his misery. "This is why friends are more trouble than they're worth. Emotions complicate shit. I don't need that in my life."

"Trust me, Callum's worth it," Jules insisted with a confidence I couldn't understand.

"Why?"

"Meet him again and figure it out yourself," he challenged me. "I'm visiting Xander at work tomorrow to drop something off for him. Why don't you come with me and invite Callum to have lunch with you? It'll give you the opportunity to apologize in person for being a dumbass with rusty social skills."

My first instinct was to reject the invitation outright, but something in me was eager to accept the contrived excuse to see Callum again.

"Give him a chance to prove your pessimism wrong. You owe him that for making him miserable these last few days wondering how he could be such an idiot for accidentally offending you somehow."

The twinge of guilt made it easier for me to agree. "Okay." The instant the words were out of my mouth, I felt lighter, even as I reminded myself not to get my hopes up about Callum. I hated being disappointed.

Chapter Five

CALLUM

I HELD in another sigh as I checked the clock again to see if it was time for my lunch break. Mustering up enthusiasm for working today was challenging. It had been four days since I had met with Rune. I thought our meeting had gone well after my initial embarrassing stumbles, but based on his silence, I guess he had a different opinion on that. I probably made him uncomfortable by being so flustered around him, but it had been almost impossible not to be a mess when he was gorgeous beyond compare.

Plus, he loved history. How was it fair that he was so handsome *and* smart? It had been fascinating learning from him, and I yearned for another opportunity to hear more about his passion. I wanted to text him about it, but it was too embarrassing. The only thing worse than not hearing from him at all would be complete silence after I reached out to him. That kind of rejection would be so much more painful. At least if I didn't message him, I could pretend he was too busy to bother with me. It was a hollow comfort, though.

"Hey, Callum!"

At the sound of Jules's cheery greeting, I turned around to face him. My initial response died on my tongue when I saw that he wasn't alone. Rune was with him, looking like sin itself in a dark gray suit, black shirt, and silver Greek key tie with blue and teal flourishes. In black-rimmed glasses, he resembled a sexy professor I desperately wanted to teach me a lesson.

It was almost impossible to tear my gaze away from Rune, but I forced myself to focus on Jules. I was proud I managed to squeak out the word "Hi," when inside I was losing my shite over Rune being there with his brother.

Jules was kind enough not to laugh at my response. "How's it going?"

"Uh, good? Yeah, good. Good is good. Great, actually. Right?" Fantastic, I sounded like an idiot in front of Rune again.

"Right," Jules agreed, amusement lacing his tone. "I'll go bug Xander now, so I'll see you around."

My heart leapt into my throat when I realized he was leaving me alone with Rune. I dared to glance up at him through lowered lashes, causing my pulse to skyrocket at how beautiful he was. How was it possible for one person to be *that* attractive? God, and he smelled *so fucking good*. Was there an aphrodisiac in his cologne? It made me want to lick his neck to see if he tasted as good as he smelled. Where did those weird thoughts keep coming from?

I knew I needed to speak so I didn't come off as a total gobshite. If I had been outgoing like my brother, it would have been easy to say, "It's great to see you again. Are you doing well?" Instead, all I got out was a breathy "Um, hi? Again. Hi. Hello. Hi again."

The corners of his mouth quirked up at my pathetic attempt at greeting him. His voice was smooth as silk as he replied, "Hello, Callum."

I hadn't known my name could be sexy until I heard Rune say it. The sound of it on his lips sent shivers through me. It made it exceedingly hard to respond, but I valiantly fought against my ineptitude. "How have you been?" I applauded myself for getting out a complete sentence. It was a serious triumph in the face of his good looks.

"It's been brought to my attention that I've been a shitty friend." He carded his fingers through his hair, making me feel faint. "I owe you yet another apology."

"Huh?" I cleared my throat and tried again for a better response. "What? Why?" Oh well, so much for those complete sentences. They were overrated, anyway.

Rune rested his forearms on the countertop of my

reception desk. "Apparently, my social skills were rustier than I thought. I should have texted you instead of waiting for you to reach out to me."

That caught me by surprise. "Oh, I assumed you were busy. I was afraid I'd annoy you, so—"

"I wouldn't have given you my personal number if I didn't want to hear from you. It's my fault for not being clear about that. In the future, please text me."

"Is it really okay?" I asked in a small voice. "I wouldn't want to be a bother, or—"

He interrupted me again. "You're not. I promise I'll also be better about reaching out. I'm sorry if my silence upset you."

My spirit soared at his apology. "No, it's fine. I assumed you didn't want to hear me blathering nonsense again."

"That couldn't be further from the truth. I'm here to invite you to join me for lunch to make it up to you."

My jaw dropped in shock. "*You* want to take *me* out?"

"I do. Is that something you'd be interested in?"

"Of course!" I remembered to rein in my enthusiasm. "Um, I mean, yeah, that would be nice. But I'm not allowed to be on break at the same time as Xander, so—"

"It's fine," Xander interrupted me as he came out of his office to drop off a stack of files at my desk. "You can go."

"How pissed are you going to be if I don't bring him back in an hour at precisely 1:16?" Rune asked him.

"Try not to turn it into a three-hour siesta, okay?"

Rune's cheeky grin made my heart flutter so fast I worried I was in danger of passing out. "I'll try, but I'm not making any promises. I'm taking him to Ambrosia."

"Tell Maria and Renée hi for me. Let them know I'll have Jules bring me there soon."

I couldn't believe my luck. "If I'm late, I'll stay later tonight to make up the time."

"That won't be necessary. Go have a fun lunch and don't worry about keeping an eye on the clock. Ambrosia should be savored and enjoyed, not rushed. You get back when you get back. If you need to take the rest of the day off, it's not the end of the world."

"Thank you." Not for the first time was I overcome by how grateful I was to have him as a boss.

Rune waved goodbye. "Enjoy my brother."

"I always do." It was comments like that which made me wonder if Xander and Jules were something more than friends.

Once we were alone, Rune asked, "Ready to go?"

I shut off my computer monitor and grabbed my phone. "Yes!" I was on cloud nine because he wanted to spend time with me, erasing my insecurity from the past few days of silence.

I NEVER UNDERSTOOD why some men were so obsessed with cars. But after riding in Rune's Italian sports car, I had a whole new appreciation for why guys lost their shite over them. Every time he wrapped his large hand around the gearshift of his vintage Ferrari, he caressed it as he slid it into position to change gears. I swallowed hard as I fought against my arousal. It was a struggle when his masculine and seductive scent filled the enclosed space, further stimulating me. I had been suffering with a semi from the moment we first rocketed down the street after leaving my office, desperately fighting against becoming fully erect.

Thanks to the loud engine that sent vibrations thrumming through my body, there wasn't much talking on the way to the restaurant. It was a relief, because the experience reduced me to wanting to whimper with need and beg him to do things to me that were too embarrassing to ask for. It was growing increasingly difficult to control my raging hormones around him.

I reminded myself I shouldn't be thinking of Rune like that. He was a friend and nothing more. I learned that the hard way with Gregory. No good ever came out of falling for your friends. It didn't matter how sexy they were.

Besides, what did an awkward virgin like me have to offer someone as gorgeous and experienced as him? At best, I could give him a good laugh over how bad I would be at everything. I was almost twenty-one and had never been kissed yet, let alone do anything beyond that. He would probably think I was pathetic, and he would be right. But it was hard to get dating experience when your da's religion kept you deep in the closet for most of your life.

As we waited at a red light, Rune absentmindedly stroked the head of the gearshift knob. It made my prick stand up at full attention, begging to be teased like that. I subtly shifted in my seat, not wanting him to notice how turned on I was. But how could I not be when I was drowning in the smell of him and watching enviously as he gave a hand job to his shifter? I was only human. That was too much temptation to resist.

I prayed that we would arrive before I made an embarrassing mess of my pants.

ONCE WE REACHED THE RESTAURANT, Rune surprised me by pulling behind it instead of parking out front with the other customers. After we got out, we approached a locked gate with a keypad next to it, where he punched in a code. The door swung open with a metallic creak, allowing him to lead the way into a sizable garden. I entered paradise as I stepped inside and stared in astonishment. There were tall trees and beautiful flowers everywhere the eye could see. An enormous fountain dominated the middle, providing a peaceful burbling that drowned out the sounds of the city outside the ivy-covered walls. Tables and chairs were scattered around the area.

"What is this place?" Somehow, we had stepped into another world and left Sunnyside behind. I had never seen such a beautiful oasis before.

"Ambrosia." Rune said that word as if that explained everything. He gestured for me to join him at a table under a pergola. It had white curtains gathered at the corners and fairy lights wrapped around the wood that must have been stunning at night. Flowers covered the trellis on top, providing shade from the afternoon sun as we sat down for lunch. With a light breeze, the weather was perfect for alfresco dining.

Before I could ask a follow-up question, a tall woman with brunette hair pulled into an updo appeared. She was a timeless beauty, who had an elegant air about her as she moved with the fluid grace of a dancer. Her floral-print wrap dress hugged her feminine curves, and her smile was as beautiful as her. "Hello and welcome. It's good to see you again, Rune. I'm loving your sexy Clark Kent look."

He took off his glasses and set them on the table,

making me mourn the loss. "Sorry, I forgot I still had those on. I wore them for his office."

She laughed at the comment, but it confused me. Why would he need to wear them only at my office? Her amusement was evident as she commented, "I can't believe that stupid trick works. But I guess if it's good enough for Superman, it's good enough for you."

"That's the idea." They exchanged air-kisses on each cheek. "Have you and Renée been well?"

"Yes, thank you. I'm happy to see you've brought a friend this time."

Rune made introductions. "Maria, this is Callum. He works for Xander. Callum, this is Maria. She's the manager of Ambrosia, and her wife, Renée, is the two Michelin-star head chef here."

"We're hoping it'll be three-star soon." She extended her hand to me. "It's a pleasure to meet you, Callum."

Her skin was so soft, it was like touching an angel. "Nice to meet you, too. I feel like I'm in heaven here."

Maria's open demeanor made it seem as if you had always known her somehow. "Once you eat, you'll be in heaven for real. Do you have any allergies or dislikes that we should avoid?"

I shook my head. "No, I'm fine with anything."

"Excellent. In that case, I'll have Renée get started on something special for you, then be back with drinks in a moment."

My confusion over the lack of a menu must have shown on my face because Rune explained, "Renée always makes a custom tasting course for me."

"It gives my wife a chance to flex and show off a little. Trust me, you're in for a genuine treat."

"I'm so excited!" That was an understatement.

She smiled at my enthusiasm before heading back inside to take care of things. Once she left, I commented, "Wow, she's so nice."

"Maria and Renée are great. You won't find better food or service anywhere in the world."

I ignored my internal pleas to not make an idiot out of myself. "Um, can I ask a weird question?"

"Sure."

"Why did you only need glasses for my office?" There wasn't a single reason I could think of for why he would only need them there.

"It's a useful trick to avoid being recognized. They alter my appearance enough that people assume I could never be me when I'm in an unexpected place. It doesn't always work, but I prefer it to everyone recognizing me and causing a big fuss."

I tilted my head as I mulled over his words. "But you didn't wear them the first time we met."

"No, I rarely bother wearing them at the Brewhaha Café since they're usually not busy. I've never been hassled there, thankfully."

"I owe you an apology for being clueless about

Fancy Love

who you are," I said. "I'll probably feel like a bloody idiot if I ever find out, won't I?"

He chuckled, sending a shiver through me. "No apologies are necessary. It's a relief to be myself around you. I assumed the only people who didn't know me were the Amish, so it was a wonderful gift."

"Even if I knew who you were, it wouldn't change how I treat you." It was important to me he understood that.

His gaze softened as he looked at me with something akin to affection, sending millions of butterflies into flight inside of me. "I know."

Maria returned with a server, bringing out our drinks and first course. "Carrie will be helping me today. To start off with, this is a parmesan budino with truffle perlage."

Carrie set the plates in front of us before she and Maria went back inside the restaurant.

In the center of the white dish was a small custard tart topped with arugula, surrounded by a ring of tiny caviar balls. I could only imagine how much it cost. It was probably the single most expensive thing I had ever eaten in my life.

Rune picked up his silverware as he encouraged me, "If you like cheese, you'll love it."

"It's so pretty, I don't think I can eat it. This isn't food; it's art!"

His amusement and delight at my reaction was

obvious. I basked in his warmth like a sunflower does in rays of sunlight. "You're not wrong."

Even though it was sacrilege to ruin something so beautiful, I cut into it and stacked a few balls of caviar on top. I wasn't sure what to expect when I put it in my mouth, but the nuttiness from the black truffles complemented the creaminess of the parmesan cheese. The perlage brought some acidity to it, while the salad kept it from being too rich. Everything was perfectly balanced into a decadent treat. I couldn't hold in my moan of appreciation. "*Wow.*" The single word was inadequate to describe how amazing the food was yet summed up my awe of the dish.

My second bite defied logic by being even better than the first. I took my time savoring each morsel, but the small budino disappeared all too soon. It was hard not to pout.

Maria and Carrie returned. "How was it?"

"Incredible!" I gushed, unable to contain my excitement.

"Amazing, as usual," Rune added. "Renée always outdoes herself."

She beamed at the praise for her wife's cooking as she collected our empty plates. "I'm so pleased you enjoyed it! Next, we have a risotto with shaved white truffle."

"She's really going all out, isn't she?" he asked in an impressed tone as Carrie set the dishes down on the table.

"Of course! I told her you brought someone, so she wanted to make it extra special for you." I blushed at the implication. "She doesn't break out the white truffles for just anyone, you know."

The creamy risotto had marbleized white truffle shavings on top. After the two women left, I took a bite. The robust flavors exploded on my tongue, leaving me in awe. "This is incredible! I didn't know food could be this good!"

Rune closed his eyes for a moment as he savored the taste. The satisfaction on his face made my cock perk up once more as the visual gave me ideas of other scenarios where he would have that kind of expression. When he opened them again, my heart skipped a beat. "Renée really is a culinary genius."

"I appreciate you bringing me here. No one's ever done anything like this for me before."

He seemed surprised by my comment. "Your boyfriend has never taken you to lunch before?"

My cheeks had to be as red as my hair. "N-no, I—I've never had a b-b-boyfriend."

"Ah, sorry. I shouldn't have assumed. Girlfriend?"

I tripped up over my words and tried not to die of embarrassment. "You were—um, right about the —about being gay. But I've never dated anyone, so…"

If I didn't know any better, I'd almost swear there was a spark of interest in his expressive blue eyes. But that wasn't possible, right? "Someone as cute as you definitely should have had men lined up fighting for a chance to be with you."

My brain boggled that somebody as handsome as him thought I was cute. "Trust me, no one was interested in me. The only person—"

"The only person? I find it hard to believe that only one person was interested in you."

"No, I was only interested in one person." I didn't want to ruin lunch with what had happened to me back then, but I never knew when to stop. "The black eye he gave me made it abundantly clear he was too straight to reciprocate my feelings."

An angry storm passed through Rune's eyes, which sent an exhilarating rush through me. His voice came out as a dark growl that did things to me I didn't understand. "Tell me you pressed charges against that asshole."

"I didn't stick around long enough to do that." Even if I had, I never would have brought myself to seek retribution against Gregory. "The shiner forced me to come out to my parents when I got home, and Da disowned me. Ma sent me here to live with my brother since it wasn't safe for me to stay with them in Ireland anymore."

"I'm so sorry. No one deserves that, especially not you."

The caring concern in his gaze was too much for me to bear. I looked away with a shrug. "It was my fault for being stupid enough to fall for someone who could never love me back."

He reached out and took my hand in his. I inhaled as the gesture once again sent electricity ricocheting through me at top speed. Every nerve in my body reacted to such a stunning man touching me. "It's never wrong to want love, Callum. You deserve to have someone love you back."

When he squeezed my hand in silent comfort, it rendered me speechless. The restaurant door opened, but Rune didn't jerk away like he had been burned. Instead, he rubbed his thumb against the back of my hand, making me tremble with want. It took effort not to cry the tears that welled up in my eyes from his gentle understanding. His touch made me yearn for so much more, but I treasured what was being offered to me.

He let go so they could clear the plates and serve the follow-up course, leaving me bereft. It gave me an unsettling urge to curl up in his embrace and soak up the comfort he was willing to offer me. In that moment, he had given me the only real solace I had found in my regrettable situation with Gregory.

Maria didn't comment on our hand holding as she introduced the next dish. "This is a ridged pasta with chicken confit marsala. Enjoy."

Despite my emotional state, I remembered to say, "Thank you."

There were three large pasta noodles on the

bottom, with two more stacked on top in the opposite direction. It was covered by a piece of chicken, all of it drenched in a rich brown marsala sauce. Grateful for an excuse to move on from the uncomfortable topic, I enjoyed the wonderful pasta that had a savory flavor. Once again, it was gone in a few bites, making me wish there was more of it. "Mm, I could eat a whole plate of that and be happy."

"That's the problem with tasting menus. You always want more of each thing. Also, I'm sorry for bringing up something so unpleasant for you earlier. That wasn't my intention."

Not wanting the mood to stay serious, I was more bold than normal. "You more than made up for it by telling me I'm cute when you look like you."

"I was merely stating the obvious."

His words made me laugh. "I really don't think it's that obvious."

"You don't think you're cute?" He quirked one perfect eyebrow up in disbelief.

"What's cute about being awkward?"

Before he replied, they interrupted us once more for the next course. He asked Maria, "Do you think Callum's cute?"

She giggled at the question as she cleared the plates. "Honey, you need to get real glasses if you can't see how adorable he is."

"Believe me, *I* know he's cute. He's the one who doesn't understand his own appeal."

"He's super precious," Carrie added. "His Irish accent earns him bonus points."

I was pretty sure my embarrassed flush went to the tips of my ears. The praise was too much to handle. I comforted myself by smoothing down the corners of my pink swirl bow tie. "I'm just me."

Maria squeezed my shoulder with her free hand. "Friendly tip: if someone as sexy as Rune tells you you're cute, believe him. He's not in the habit of praising people unless they deserve it."

"But…" My protest died because I didn't know what I was trying to say.

Carrie placed the new dishes down, which looked like finely shaved bright green ice.

"This is a palate cleanser of vanilla-rose Chantilly cream, apple and wasabi granita, with blueberries," Maria informed us. "You're going to love it."

"Did you say *wasabi*?" I never expected there to be Japanese ingredients at an Italian restaurant.

Maria grinned. "I sure did. Enjoy."

After she left with Carrie, Rune asked, "Do you believe me now?"

"I think you're all being very nice." It was impossible to wrap my mind around him feeling that way about me.

"If I didn't know any better, I'd say that was a challenge for me to convince you."

The words escaped me before I could stop them. "How would you do that?"

His knowing smirk made my pants grow tight as his blue eyes blazed with a heat that melted me into a quivering puddle. "Oh, I have my ways."

I *really* hoped some of those ways involved being pinned down in bed. The thought startled me. After repressing my reactions to men for so long, I wasn't used to being so reactively horny. I wished I was suave enough to invite him to give it a shot, but I couldn't bring myself to say it. "I'm not sure if I'd survive that."

"I bet you're more resilient than you think."

His words did nothing to lessen my throbbing need for him to convince me in graphic detail. Rather than embarrassing myself by responding further, I focused on trying the beautiful granita. The vanilla-rose Chantilly cream tempered the tartness of the apple and the kick of the wasabi. The blueberries added a burst of sweetness that once again amazed me at how balanced the flavor profiles were. I had never had such an impressive meal in my life.

When Rune moaned because of the refreshing dish, my heart stuttered in my chest. He looked downright orgasmic, which sent my arousal into overdrive. If I didn't get things under control soon, he'd see cartoon steam coming out of my ears. I hated thinking about my friend like that, but Rune was making it impossible not to imagine being in bed together.

He locked gazes with me, causing my breathing to hitch. I trembled under the intensity of his blue eyes, which conveyed sexual things there was no way he could ever mean with me. A high-pitched squeak escaped me. His expression turned predatory, almost as if he wanted to devour me next for dessert. I thought my heart would explode out of my chest like a burning sun. Were truffles an aphrodisiac? That was the only excuse for why my desire was running rampant with lust and imaging he would be interested in me.

"How good was that granita?" Maria asked.

I startled, having been so entranced by Rune that I hadn't noticed her or Carrie return.

Unflappable, Rune replied, "The wasabi was an unexpected surprise, but really worked, though."

"You know how Renée is. She's adventurous about everything."

The two shared a look that conveyed the innuendo wasn't lost on him. "She's quite the intrepid explorer."

"Lucky me, I always get the benefit," Maria teased, causing Carrie to snicker beside her. "Anyway, this dessert is one of my personal favorites. We're going full decadent with a white truffle gelato, sea salt cocoa crumb, and shaved chocolate."

Visually, the dish lacked the refinement of the others, but it still looked delectable. The ice cream was more yellow than vanilla, standing out against the brown of the chocolate shavings covering it and the bottom of the bowl.

"I didn't know it was possible to make gelato out of truffles," I commented in surprise.

"Oh, Renée *loves* pushing the boundaries of what she can put in gelato. But I drew the line at her squid ink gelato."

"*Squid ink?*"

"Yeah, it was as gross as it sounds." Maria wrinkled her nose at the memory. "I don't care what she says. Gelato shouldn't have umami flavors."

Rune shook his head. "I trust her with almost anything, but I'm not sure if I could stomach that."

"Thankfully, this is much better by miles. I'll leave you to it."

"Thanks." I was eager to dive into my favorite part of any meal. The hint of truffle in the gelato was subtle, but the salt in the cocoa crumb enhanced the sweetness of the dessert. It paired well with the dark chocolate. "I need to learn some new adjectives, because it's not enough to say this is divine."

"Mm, Renée's outdone herself again."

I tried not to squirm while watching the spoon slide between his lips as he sucked the gelato off it. Lusting after him was a shitty way to repay him for taking me to the best lunch of my life. "Thank you for this incredible experience."

"I'm glad you're having a good time." His eyes were bright with pleasure, looking even more beautiful than the blue sky above us. How was that possible? "I am, too."

It was poor form to scrape the bowl with the spoon, but that didn't stop me from enjoying every drop of the gelato. "Although thanks to this, you've ruined normal food forever."

I loved hearing his unrestrained amusement as he chuckled. It drew me to him like a moth to a flame.

There hadn't been many perfect days in my life, but this was up there for one of the best.

Chapter Six

RUNE

HOW DID Callum not understand he was cute? In his gray suit, lavender shirt, and pink swirl bow tie, he could have been the portrait alongside the definition of the word "cute" in the dictionary. He also was the poster child for the boy next door people dreamed of falling in love with.

But it wasn't only his sweet face. His genuine enthusiasm for everything was adorable. Watching him coo about Renée's delicious cooking was precious. It had been such a long, long time since I had met someone who took that much pleasure in small things. Not to mention the fact that his gentle Irish brogue would be considered swoon-worthy by most people. I certainly couldn't get enough of listening to it.

Beyond that, I couldn't comprehend how somebody as kind and good-looking as Callum had never dated before. He seemed like the type who still believed in true love, so it made sense that he didn't have a lot of exes. But to have never been with anyone defied logic.

The only thing more baffling was that the only man Callum had liked had decked him for it. I wasn't a violent person by nature, but damned if hearing that didn't make me want to exact retribution on his behalf. Watching the light dim in his eyes as he blamed himself for loving the wrong guy brought out an unfamiliar urge to protect him. He was just some kid who worked with Xander. So why did knowing that happened to him fill me with a need to gather him up into a tight hug? I *hated* hugging.

As a lifelong introvert who had no close friends, I wasn't used to offering comfort in the face of something terrible. But I had given in to my strange desire to reach out to him, to comfort him with my touch and tell him he deserved love I didn't believe existed. I should have had no problem staying out of it or letting my cynicism tell him that most men were unworthy assholes. Yet, for some inexplicable reason, I had been compelled to offer him hope. Why had I done that? And why had seeing his joy return loosen a tightness in my chest and fill me with relief? It made no damn sense. Why should his happiness matter to me at all?

Our next interruption came in the form of Renée, the talented Michelin-star chef who had prepared our wonderful lunch. She was shorter than her wife and rougher around the edges, but she had the same accepting heart as Maria. Her blond hair was shaved on the sides and left long on top in rainbow stripes. Tattoos covered both of her arms and hands, as well as her neck. Renée's life had been tough growing up, so I admired her for fighting against the odds and living her dream of running a famous restaurant. She tended to give me shit, but it was all in good fun. The couple were the closest thing to real friends that I had outside of my brother and Xander.

Even better, she was carrying my all-time favorite drink that I had been a little sad we hadn't been served earlier. She grinned at me. "Did you really think I'd let you leave without one of these?"

"You wouldn't be you if you did," I replied. She set the tall glasses down in front of Callum and me, before giving my shoulder a firm squeeze in greeting. I appreciated that although she was a hugger, she always respected my boundaries. "Callum, this is Renée."

His face lit up in excitement as he shook her hand. He held on to it as he complimented her. "Thank you for the best meal I've had in my entire life! I'm sorry I don't know enough words to describe how delicious everything was."

"I'm thrilled you enjoyed it so much."

"I never knew food could be art until today." He looked up at her in amazement. "It was magical."

Renée fluffed up under the praise. "Damn, Maria and Carrie are right. You're absolutely adorable."

"No, I'm not." His blush came back in full force. He straightened his bow tie nervously, which was yet another adorable habit of his.

"Oh, you must have so much fun with that." Renée winked at me. "I bet if I keep complimenting him, he'll be as red as the drinks."

"Probably. Thank you for these, by the way." I deserved an award for not drinking it the second she set it on the table.

Eager to get away from being the topic of conversation, Callum asked, "What are they?"

"Rune's favorite drink in the world. Raspberry peach Italian cream soda. It's club soda, some raspberry and peach flavoring, whipped cream, topped off with a peach slice and whole raspberries."

He stared at the red fizzy drink topped with white cream tinged pink from the syrups. There were three raspberries on top and a peach slice on the rim of the glass, and a rainbow chrome metal straw. "That sounds wonderful. May I try it?"

She gestured for him to help himself.

Callum pulled the glass closer to him and took a sip. I had to hide a grin behind my hand at how happy his noise of delight was as he tasted it for the first time. He stared at her like she had performed an impressive magic trick. "Wow! This. Is. *Amazing!*"

"Now you know why it's Rune's fav." Renée

leaned against my chair and tugged on my earlobe. "Quit being stoic and enjoy yours, too."

I loved the drink too much to grumble about her comment. Even though she had shared her recipe with me, it always tasted better when she made it. I savored my first sip. "You outdid yourself today. Lunch was spectacular."

"Well, when I heard you brought your boyfriend here to show off, I didn't want to disappoint."

It wasn't worth making a scene to correct her. "You're incapable of cooking a disappointing meal." I had yet to try something she made that wasn't next-level delicious.

Callum almost choked on his drink. "I-I-I'm n-not his b-b-boyfriend." The charming blush from earlier began creeping up his neck and ears. "We're just friends! I work with Xander."

Renée snorted at his protests. "Do you seriously think he brings Xander's other coworkers here? I bet he couldn't name one other person who works in that office other than the owner."

"You'd win that bet." I had never had a reason to be interested in Xander's job until Callum came into my life.

"As if there were any doubts about that." Renée snickered, before turning her attention back to him. "You're the only person he's brought here besides his brother and Xander, so you're obviously important."

"No, I'm nobody special," he protested. For some reason, his comment bothered me.

Renée poked me. "I know you're the strong and silent type, but you need to do a better job of telling him he matters to you. Don't make him read in between your bullshit and guess whether coming here translates into your love language. Use your words."

I raised an eyebrow at her. "*Love language?*"

She gave me a stern look. "So, are you going to lie to me, or are you that deep in denial?"

Before I answered, Maria came out to join us. Renée called out to her, "Can you believe Rune is denying how he feels about this guy?"

"Yep, one hundred percent."

Callum became indignant. "He's not lying! This is only the second time we've met."

It intrigued me that he showed his backbone by coming to my defense. I would have assumed he was too shy to assert something so boldly, let alone to two strangers. It was interesting that he felt the need to defend me at all.

"Seriously?" Maria asked in surprise.

"We only met four days ago."

Renée doubled over with laughter, causing her wife to sigh in fond exasperation. "Be nice."

"They don't know!"

"I definitely don't know what you're carrying on about," I said, taking the opportunity to eat the peach slice off the edge of my glass.

She contained her amusement. "Then why did you bring him here?"

"The privacy the garden offers."

"Bullshit. What's the real reason?"

I crossed my arms over my chest. "Since when do you fish for compliments? You know there aren't any chefs in town who are better than you."

She stared me down as she asked with emphasis, "What's the *real* reason?"

My first instinct was to protest I had no clue what she was talking about, but the truth kept me silent. Deep down, I wanted to impress Callum, and I was confident Renée would blow his mind. I wished he would associate his awe over her cooking with me. Why the fuck did I want that? What difference did it make to me if he thought I was impressive? Since when did I show off for anybody? Let alone a twenty-year-old kid? What did I get out of that besides some unnecessary ego stroking?

Renée pulled me from my thoughts. "I stand by my earlier assertion. He's too pure and you're too old for that guessing game bullshit, Rune."

"I think I heard Carrie call for you," Maria told her wife, even though it was an obvious lie. "You should get back to the kitchen."

"No rest for the wicked, right?" Renée kissed her, then addressed Callum. "It was great meeting you. I look forward to seeing you next time. Remember, don't be afraid to call Rune on his bullshit. Sometimes he can't help it."

He diplomatically sidestepped the advice. "Thank you again for the best meal of my life."

Maria bent down to air-kiss Callum's cheeks. "Don't worry, I'll make sure he brings you back, cutie."

Renée came over to squeeze my shoulder once more. She said soft enough for my ears only, "Take it from someone who has been where you are and cares about you. Just because you've always been alone, doesn't mean you need to stay that way. The risk that scares you the most is the one worth taking. Trust me. I wouldn't have Maria otherwise."

Even though her insistence that Callum meant more to me than he did was annoying, I liked the woman too much to hold it against her. "Thank you for everything, Renée. Oh, and Xander said he'll make sure Jules brings him here soon."

"See, your brother is a prime example of how denying what you want most keeps you from what you need. Remember, that's not genetic with you two; that's stupidity. You're smart enough to avoid that. Got it?"

"Loud and clear."

She left with a last wave. Maria came over to kiss me goodbye next, but she surprised me when she whispered, "Sometimes we know before we know. Don't talk yourself out of the best thing to happen to you." She patted my cheek with a fond smile, before walking back into the restaurant.

Left alone with Callum, I waited for his reaction to what had happened. He took a long sip of his drink, before asking, "Do you know them because you come here often?"

I tried to figure out a way of explaining my connection without using language that would reveal my career. "Maria and I met through someone we both worked with." The truth was, she used to be a model, and we'd had the same agent. He put us in touch when she left the industry to help her wife start the restaurant. "Renée and I bonded over our shared love for food, and she's been kind enough to give me a few cooking lessons over the years."

His jaw dropped. "Wait, are you telling me you can cook like this, too?"

I chuckled at his reaction. "As much as I would love to boast about being anywhere close to her level, I'm still an amateur compared to her. But I can hold my own in a kitchen, yeah."

"Is there anything you can't do?" He looked at me as if I was a magical unicorn he couldn't believe existed. Why did that make my ego purr with satisfaction?

"Geometry. I was so bad at that in high school, my teacher lost her religion trying to figure out how to teach me."

Callum sighed in commiseration. "Same. I'm the

worst with numbers. No matter how hard I studied, it never made a difference. Math is a language I never learned to speak."

"That's a great way of putting it." I'd have to remember that phrase to use for myself later.

"Oh, speaking of studying." He brightened with eagerness. "After our talk at the café, I went home and read a biography about Olympe de Gouges."

The information floored me, as did his palpable enthusiasm. He had to be joking, right? What in the world would have possessed him to do such a thing? "You—you did?"

"Yeah, it was so engrossing that I read it cover to cover in a single sitting. You weren't kidding when you said she was a fascinating woman. I also started a book on the French Revolution after that, but it's long, so I haven't finished it yet."

It felt like the browser in my brain had gotten hung up, with the little spinning pinwheel of death circling endlessly. What would make Callum read *multiple books* about the area I studied? "Why did you read them?"

"I didn't realize how interesting the French Revolution was until you talked about it. I wanted to find out more," he said, before shyly adding, "and I hoped we could talk about it if we met up again. It was fun learning about what you studied."

"But I rambled about death tolls." I had gone embarrassingly deep into grim, off-putting details.

Yet, here he was, sitting across from me, not only telling me he had fun *but meant it*. That shouldn't have been possible. "And the guillotine!"

He nudged a raspberry with his straw. "I liked seeing the real you. And I…" He trailed off, then took a deep breath before forcing himself to continue. "I felt like that you might actually be interested in being friends with somebody like me. I didn't stand a chance with the other you."

My heart squeezed so tightly in my chest that I pressed my hand over it to soothe it. In a single meeting, Callum had discovered the real me I kept hidden away from everyone, and that was the part of me he liked the most. He didn't care that I was attractive; he didn't know I was a famous model, nor was he interested in the carefully crafted persona I used to sell myself to others. No, he was drawn to my inner dork who thought late-eighteenth-century France was the most fascinating period in history.

Not only that, but he educated himself to talk to me about my research. In my entire life, no one had ever shown that level of interest in what I cared about. I couldn't process that Callum wasn't saying pretty words about what he thought I wanted to hear. Somehow, he wasn't pretending to like it to impress me or get into my bed. He genuinely wanted to learn more about something I was passionate about so he could share that with me as a friend.

I had to be the biggest idiot in the world. While I

had been busy ignoring him and assuming the worst, he had been reading history books to relate to me better. He was offering me an invitation to indulge in a side of myself I rarely got to enjoy anymore. That was a gift no one had ever offered me before.

But then the other part of what he said echoed in my mind. *I felt like that you might actually be interested in being friends with somebody like me. I didn't stand a chance with the other you.* Knowing I caused him to experience that kind of hope and rejection all at once made me feel like a terrible person.

Shit, Renée was right. Callum was too pure, and I didn't deserve that kindness after the way I had treated him. I couldn't undo how I'd acted in the past, but I could damn sure make more of an effort moving forward.

In my prolonged silence as I sorted through my overwhelming surge of emotions, he grew insecure and looked away in shame. "Sorry, that's weird and probably sounds desperate, and—"

"No. Callum, I—it's not—I just—" I took a pause to breathe, needing a moment to collect myself. "Please don't apologize for doing the nicest thing anyone's ever done for me."

"You're not upset?"

"Upset?" How could he think I would be upset by what he did? That's when Renée's words from before about expressing myself rang through my mind. Damn, why was she always right? "No, I'm not upset.

I'm overwhelmed and deeply moved that you would do that. You caught me off guard, but in a good way."

The fear left him, but he still seemed uncertain. "Really?"

Like before, I didn't resist when I had the urge to reassure him with a touch. I reached out once more and took his hand in mine. The physical connection between us soothed something inside of me. "Callum, you have to understand, absolutely *no one* in my life cares about history. Nobody I work with even knows I'm interested in the subject. My brother hated school. My parents are engineers. History is my weird quirk that they put up with. They don't know that Olympe existed, nor would they care."

"How could you not care about someone whose philosophy was 'I'm determined to be a success, and I'll do it in spite of my enemies'?"

Waves of disbelief and gratitude crashed over me again. He'd not only read about Olympe, but he remembered quotes of things she said in her writings? I stared at him, awestruck. How was it possible for him to be *that* sincere in his interest?

Reacting on instinct, I interlocked our fingers, allowing me to squeeze his hand. His was smaller than mine, fitting perfectly like he was created for me. It filled me with an unfamiliar warmth and a longing to pull him into my lap so I could embrace him. Why did I keep having that urge when I despised hugging?

It normally made me feel trapped and claustrophobic, so why did I want to reach out to him and hold him close?

It was a struggle to express myself, but I forced myself to try for his sake. "I never expected anyone to care about a side of me that most people don't even know exists, let alone attempt to relate to me on that level."

"But that's so lonely."

His comment made me remember my brother asking me if I understood that I was lonely. I had scoffed at the time, but it was hard to deny. It *was* lonely always being cut off from the only part of myself that still felt genuine joy. And here was beautiful Callum, offering me a chance to be happy again by letting me be the real me I had to hide from everyone else. I meant it more than I ever thought possible when I told him, "It's not now that you're here."

With his radiant smile, he burrowed deep inside my thawing heart. For the first time in my life, I didn't stop that from happening. On instinct, I brought our intertwined hands and placed a kiss on the back of his. He didn't understand what a gift he had given me, but I was grateful he had come into my life to make it better.

Chapter Seven

CALLUM

IT HAD BEEN a week since my amazing lunch with Rune at Ambrosia. Every time I remembered that afternoon, a giddy bubble of joy welled up inside of me. My heart always started beating a little faster at the memory of how he held my hand and looked at me with such genuine emotions. It had been nerve-racking, but the result was that he opened up and let me see who he really was.

Thankfully, Xander had been understanding about me not returning to the office afterward. Rune and I had stayed in the garden and chatted for hours, unaware that time had passed. It was only once the sun started setting that we realized I had missed the rest of the workday.

We had texted every day since, and I never once got the impression I was bothering him. It had been fun sending him my reactions to the history book I was reading on the French Revolution. His dry sense of humor could be a little tricky to decipher sometimes, but I was getting better at understanding him.

Earlier in the evening, I came across a line in the text I wanted to mention to Rune. However, I didn't have the chance to do it before dinner with my brother and his boyfriend.

I enjoyed hanging out with Brody and Augie, who never made me feel like an awkward third wheel. We existed in harmony as a proper family, which meant everything to me after being rejected by Da for who I was. I wished Ma had also moved to America, but she loved her new single life at her apartment after her divorce.

A lot of nights, Augie's younger brother, Felix, would come over and we would hang out and have a great night together. It was only the three of us tonight, though. After finishing dinner, we moved to the living room and started watching a movie.

It was rude to pull out my phone, but I couldn't resist the urge to text Rune before it got too late.

> Why would anyone bury a term as amazing as "revolutionary erotic libel" in a footnote?

I didn't expect an immediate response, but I felt better having sent the message. hopefully, he would find it as amusing as I did.

Much to my surprise, my phone almost immediately vibrated as the notification came through that he replied. My eyes went wide at what I saw.

> RUNE
>
> Are you flirting with me?

I could imagine his little half-smirk while teasing me. The first thing that popped into my head was to type, *Is it working?* However, I wasn't that bold. After five deleted tries to answer his simple question, I settled for a more neutral response.

> Is that how flirting works? I wouldn't know.

That much was true. I had zero experience in flirting with anyone, let alone seducing them. The very idea of me being suave enough to intrigue Rune on that level was laughable.

I eagerly watched the three flashing dots, wondering how he would reply.

> RUNE
>
> I guess it depends on what direction you intend to take this conversation.

I debated for a moment on how to respond. My self-preservation instincts that begged me not to embarrass myself were telling me to abort the conversation in favor of a safer topic. But the curious part of my brain won out.

Fancy Love

> I didn't realize erotica had the power to bring down a queen like Marie Antoinette.

As soon as I hit Send, I immediately wished I hadn't. I was daft for bringing up erotica to him. My fingers itched to type something to diffuse the strangeness of my comment, but his reply came through too fast.

RUNE
> A lot of it was straight up pornography, actually.

Heat crept to my cheeks from reading the word "pornography." After growing up in a very repressed Irish Catholic family, I hadn't been comfortable enough with my sexuality to brave watching porn on the internet. It had terrified me Da would find out somehow and kick me out of the house. Turns out he did that without the offending pornography.

Now that I was free from his influence, it still seemed too embarrassing to watch. It made me too self-conscious to get off on the voyeurism of other people's pleasure, killing any trace of my arousal.

I glanced up at Brody and Augie curled up together on the couch. My paranoia told me that somehow, they would know I was talking about porn with Rune, albeit from the eighteenth century rather than contemporary. Thankfully, their attention was on the screen, but my heart yearned for the tender intimacy they shared. Augie nestled against Brody's side, using his shoulder as a headrest. My brother had his arm around his boyfriend, holding him close as they cuddled. I had never experienced that in my life. It was hard not to feel like I was missing out.

Once I realized they were watching the movie and not me, I remembered that I hadn't answered yet. I hurriedly typed back.

> I'm not sure I understand the difference.

RUNE

> Pornography is filthier. People had a vivid imagination in those days, especially considering the internet was centuries away from existing.

> What do you mean?

Ugh, how many more embarrassing ways could I prove I was a virgin in a single conversation with Rune? It was in those moments I became overly conscious of our ten-year age gap and sexual experiences.

> **RUNE**
>
> Drawing Marie Antoinette having sex with a woman or a man was an unimaginative and common way of sullying her reputation. I'm talking about the artists who took pornography to a different dimension of weird fuckery.

His description piqued my curiosity. I needed to know more, although my cheeks were flame red in secondhand embarrassment.

> The book only showed a picture plate from a libelle pamphlet of Marie Antoinette kissing a woman. They both were wearing fancy dresses, so it's a far cry from obscene.

> **RUNE**
>
> I could show you my favorite depraved one, but I don't want to get in trouble for corrupting you.

The thought of *Please corrupt me* broadsided me at a dizzying speed. Where did *that* come from? I ignored it, responding before I could talk myself out of it.

> I'm a virgin, not a minor, thank you very much.

The three dots flashed for a few moments before disappearing. It made me feel like an even bigger idiot. I wished there was a way to unsend stupid messages.

One minute dragged into two, then five, then thirty. I tried to make myself watch the movie instead of checking my screen, but I was dying inside. Surely, I had to be the dumbest arsehole in the world for sending him a text reminding him I was so young and inexperienced.

I was still beating myself up when he finally wrote back. Now, I was almost too scared to look at his message.

> **RUNE**
>
> Sorry, work called. I couldn't get him off the phone until I agreed to do a project. As I was saying, the image may be too much for your sensitive virgin eyes.

Relief flooded through me that the delay had been something normal like a work phone call and not because my reply was daft. However, my indignation over the latter part of his text smarted.

> Nice try, but my eyes aren't the part of me that is a virgin. I would think you of all people would know the difference.

I reread my message after sending it. Wait, *was I* flirting with Rune? No, there was no chance me being this awkward could be misconstrued as flirting.

> **RUNE**
> I hate to break it to you, but if you've never seen an erect dick in person that wasn't yours, your eyes are as virginal as the rest of you.

A strangled noise escaped from my throat when I read his words, which I tried to cover with a cough. My brother glanced over at me questioningly, but I shrugged and took a long drink of lemonade to cool off. I was overheated and flushed from the direction the conversation had taken.

> **RUNE**
> Am I wrong?

I wanted to brag I had seen loads of pricks in person, but he'd be able to see right through that flimsy lie. What I needed to do was quit talking to him about genitalia before mine made its presence known while I was in the same room as Brody and Augie. What I actually did was the complete opposite.

> Look, are you going to send me an eighteenth-century dick pic or not?

Before I could delete my idiotic response, I accidentally hit Send. *Fuckfuckfuckfuckfuckingfuck!*

As I continued to die of mortification over what I sent, he replied.

RUNE

Don't say I didn't warn you.

The message was followed up by the funniest picture I had ever seen in my life. Marie Antoinette was standing on the left, her hand resting on the shaft of an enormous dick-beast. The creature had the legs and hooves of a horse attached to fuzzy bollocks, where a man in uniform carrying roses sat astride them for a saddle. His sword hung down at his side as he straddled the enormously tall phallus, with the happy trail as a long tail. The blue reins he used to control it resembled the thick vein on the underside and wrapped around the tip. Most outrageous of all was the prick ejaculating spunk in front of a flying cherub holding a flaming torch and two laurel wreaths.

I laughed so hard tears came out of my eyes as I dropped my phone. Out of everything I had been expecting, a man riding a penis-horse hybrid in the middle of nutting next to a naked baby with wings had *definitely* not been anywhere on my list of possibilities.

Brody and Augie looked over at me as I wiped my eyes. "Sorry, I saw a—" *Don't say dick-beast, don't say dick-beast, don't effing say it!* "I saw a—uh, a thing. On the internet. What do you call them? A meme! Yeah, it was a meme. About the French Revolution. Heads will roll. It was a guillotine joke about capitalism and

Fancy Love 93

the rich. Very funny." I applauded myself for coming up with that absolute load of rubbish so fast.

Augie chuckled at my explanation for my outburst. "I didn't know that was a thing."

"Everything is a meme now," Brody replied.

"Sorry, I didn't mean to interrupt the movie." I picked my phone up off the floor from where I dropped it in my laughing fit.

"Don't worry about it." My older brother reminded me, "You know you're allowed to go out with Rune if you want to, right?"

It didn't surprise me he had figured out who I was texting with. "It's too late now, maybe next weekend."

"I think it would be good for you," Augie added. The show of support was nice. He had become like a second older brother to me over the past few months of living together.

"Mm-hmm."

Once they both resumed watching the movie, I checked my phone again.

> RUNE
> I scared you off, didn't I?

> Sorry, I was laughing so hard I couldn't see the screen through the tears in my eyes. What IS that thing?

> A man riding a dick the wrong way, obviously.

His words sent a visual flash of me riding him the

right way, causing my cock to stiffen with interest. I shied away from the mental image. No, I refused to fantasize about him. I never dared to imagine having sex with Gregory, so why had I pictured something so explicitly sexual with Rune?

Because you have eyes, and he is the sexiest man in the galaxy, my brain not-so-helpfully reminded me. Gregory was a troll in comparison. It was objectively true, but I wouldn't fall into that trap. One of the reasons Rune didn't have many friends was probably because they all tried to hook up with him. I wouldn't be that person.

Refocusing myself, I ignored my hard-on and wrote back to him.

> I can see that, but why a dick-beast?

RUNE
> Why not? That's absurdist eighteenth-century porn for you.

> Did people really get off on that?

> Probably.

> How did you discover that existed?

> I have a tendency of going deep down into rabbit holes. That's just one of the many, many weird and wonderful things from that time period.

My fingers hovered over the keys as I debated whether to type my next message. Rune had made it a point to assure me I could ask for his attention. He had been so generous with texting me I felt guilty asking for more, but I *really* wanted to see him again. The picture he sent would have been so much better to laugh about together in-person.

I forced myself to be brave, knowing it was now or never.

> Do you think we could meet sometime and talk about what you found down some of those rabbit holes? I'm curious.

RUNE
I'd love to say tomorrow, but I'm leaving at 4:45 for a business trip in the morning. Does Saturday next week work for you?

It was impossible to restrain my pleased grin. He'd *love* to say tomorrow and offered me a weekend date? Well, not a *date*-date, but still. I'd get to see him again soon, which was the only thing that mattered.

RUNE
Since I'm making you wait, I'll cook dinner to make it up to you.

If my smile grew any wider, my face would split in half. I had to bite my lip to hold in the excited squeal at the thought of getting to taste his cooking. It was sure to be amazing because everything about him was.

> I would love that if it's not too much trouble.

RUNE
> Between the two of us, I'm the one who's trouble.

> Why?

> I just sent you a dick pic from the 1780s and you need to ask why I'm trouble?

> Maybe I want to get in trouble.

Damn it, why had I sent that? What was I trying to do? Bloody hell, my excitement over getting to see him soon scrambled my brain.

RUNE
> So you ARE flirting with me.

> I don't know what I'm doing.

Well, that much was at least true. I didn't indeed understand what type of trouble I was asking for.

Yes, you do, the naughty voice in my mind whispered.

I shoved it back into its box in the dusty corners of my brain as I denied, *No. I. Do. Not!* It was hard to ignore the echoing snicker that didn't believe me at all.

> RUNE
> You're being a tease.

It wasn't intentional! It just sort of…happened. I knew it was wrong, but it also was exhilarating. It left me on the edge of my seat waiting to see how he would respond.

> Sorry, I didn't mean to.

> RUNE
> I didn't say it was a bad thing.

I read and reread his words at least a hundred times before I could manage a response.

> It's not?

The three dots blipped over and over before disappearing. They came back, then went away again. When they returned a third time, I wondered what he could be typing.

> RUNE
> No.

I raised my eyebrows in surprise. All of that typing and I only received *no*? What had he been trying to tell me before he thought better of it? I worried my lower lip between my teeth. The smart thing would be to leave it alone. But as I had proven several times during the conversation, I was anything but smart. Why act like a genius now?

> Wow, that was a LOT of typing for such a short answer.

When he didn't reply, I got nervous, but stubbornly doubled down.

> What did you really want to say?

RUNE
Something I know better than to tell you.

He was killing me with suspense. What did *that* mean? My heart was racing as I tried to find out more.

> Which is?

It took so long for the responding dots to show up, I worried I had pushed too hard. But finally, his answer came through.

RUNE
You're not ready for that kind of trouble.

> When will I be?

Maybe never.

I frowned at his text. That was unsatisfying, not to mention unhelpful.

> What if I ask nicely?

RUNE

Who asks nicely for trouble?

> Someone like me who was raised with good manners. May I pretty please have some trouble, sir?

Once again, the dots danced on my screen and toyed with my anxiety.

RUNE

It's surprisingly hard to tell you no.
Especially when you call me "sir."

> Then don't tell me no. Problem solved, sir.

Huh, I apparently got ballsy whenever I was denied after teasing. Who knew? I'd be more embarrassed about it, but the game was too much fun to play with him. Our banter gave me an addictive rush unlike anything I had experienced before.

RUNE

It's a no for now. Satisfied?

> No, not at all.

Good, then that makes two of us.

I scratched my head as I tried to decode his cryptic comment. Why would he be unsatisfied? If he wanted to tell me yes, then why wouldn't he? And what were we even talking about now?

Don't act like you don't know, the whisper inside me taunted, a flicker of my graphic vision from before flashing in my mind.

Absolutely not. I refused to listen to my inner… whatever the hell was being so obnoxious.

> RUNE
> Promise me one thing?

> Sure.

> Two things, actually.

> Okay.

> One, don't agree to promises with someone like me without hearing what's being requested first. That'll get you into the wrong kind of trouble.

> As opposed to the right kind of trouble? What's that?

> Maybe we'll talk about that later. Two, will you text me while I'm gone on my business trip?

My annoyance over being denied again was overtaken by a warm fuzzy feeling at his second request. I would have been too worried about bothering him while he was away working to message him, so having him ask helped alleviate my worries about being annoying.

> You really want me to?

RUNE

Hearing from you every day would make me very happy.

I once again had to hold in a delighted noise. It blew my mind that I could make him happy. I kept expecting to wake up and discover everything had been a wonderful dream.

> It would make me happy, too.

After rereading my text, I hurried to correct my mistake.

> I mean, talking to you every day would make me happy. Not that hearing from me every day would make me happy. You know what I mean.

RUNE

I do. I'm going to get some sleep now since my flight is early. I'll talk to you tomorrow after I land in New York. Thanks for ending my night on a good (and slightly pervy) note.

> Sweet dreams.

> Same to you. Although, I apologize in advance if a wild dick-beast crashes your nightmares tonight. Or any other night, really.

I laughed out loud, grinning like an idiot at my screen.

> If it does, you'll be hearing about it.

> RUNE
> God, I sure hope so. The more graphic details, the better.

> Thanks for corrupting me (and possibly my dreams) tonight.

> I'll try not to make it a habit.

> I won't complain if you do.

> Good to know. Night.

> Good night.

With our conversation over, I set my phone aside and basked in the gushing feelings over how my night had turned out. Perhaps it was weird I was starting to mention things to Rune that were better left unsaid, but it didn't seem to bother him. If anything, he seemed kind of into it? Maybe? Or was I deluding myself? It was hard to tell when I had no frame of reference.

"You like him."

I stiffened at my brother's amused observation,

feeling like they had caught me doing something wrong. Which was absurd, since there was nothing wrong with texting a friend, or being twenty years old and talking about dick-beasts and eighteenth-century porn, for that matter. Wasn't that what all guys did?

Trying to play it cool, I shrugged. "He's my friend. Of course I like him."

"Not that type of like."

I sounded very prim when I denied, "I have no idea what you're talking about."

"Uh-huh, sure. Why else would you spend the entire movie grinning at your phone like you were texting your first boyfriend?"

My indignation flared. "I did not!" When Augie smothered his laugh, I glanced at the television to prove my point, only to discover the movie was over and the TV was off. So much for that defense. "Okay, fine! Maybe I did. So what?"

Brody's fond look disarmed my defensiveness. "It's not a bad thing. I think it's great."

"It's not great. It's terrible!"

"What's terrible?"

Guilt and anxiety mixed in my stomach as I said out loud what I wished I didn't think. "The last time I fell for my best friend, I lost him, my dignity, and my home. I won't go through that again!"

"C'mere, Cally." He gestured for me to come closer.

I dutifully went over to stand beside the couch.

He stared up at me with unwavering affection that moved me in the face of my fears. "You'll *never* lose your home again because I love you and you're my brother. Nothing will ever make me send you away. I'm not Da. More than anything, I want you to find happiness like I have with Augie with your own boyfriend someday."

"I haven't known Rune that long, but I don't want to lose him because I was stupid and fell for him." My heart clenched in my chest at the thought of him disappearing from my life.

"Gregory was a fucking idiot and didn't deserve you." Brody still held a deep grudge against my former best friend for hitting me when he found out about my crush. "Rune is obviously different."

"I don't know if he's gay. He's never said he is or talked about having partners before. But someone as gorgeous as him surely has been with a ton of people."

Augie shrugged. "If he's as introverted as you said, maybe not."

"No, you don't get it. I'm not exaggerating; he's literally the most beautiful person on this planet. If you ever meet him, you'll understand."

"We want to. Bring him over here sometime, even just as a friend."

"It'll be like when Felix comes over," Augie agreed.

I didn't feel right asking Rune to come hang out

with my family when we weren't dating. Plus, there was a selfish part of me that wanted to keep him to myself for a little longer. "Perhaps someday. I think I'll take a shower and go to bed, though."

Brody got up and hugged me. Since he was much taller than me and made of massive muscles, being held by him really made me feel like his baby brother. I was grateful for the love and acceptance that he offered me. "Cally, I love you, no matter what."

"I know." After our religious upbringing, I never took it for granted that he felt that way. "I love you, too."

Brody pulled back and ruffled my hair with a warm smile. "Good lad. Go get some sleep."

After wishing them good night, I got ready to take my shower. Once I was alone in the glass stall, I relaxed as the hot water warmed me. I hadn't realized how on edge my conversation with Rune had made me until then. But it was weird because it wasn't in a bad way. It had been fun, exhilarating, and weirdly erotic. It shouldn't have surprised me since everything about Rune was sexual.

I replayed our conversation in my mind as I washed off and shampooed my hair. If I didn't know any better—and I certainly didn't—I would almost swear he was flirting back with me. But what sense did that make? He had no incentive to flirt with me when I was, well, *me*.

Half of me regretted how bold I was while

texting, while the other part of me wished I had pushed things further. Then again, if I was a person who could ask if Rune meant the sexy kind of trouble, he would have a reason to pursue me. That had to be what he meant, right? But what was sexy about an inexperienced virgin who barely knew his arsehole from his elbow? Even in the unlikely event Rune *was* interested in me, all I would do is embarrass myself with him.

But he could teach you.

Wow, that whisper was getting *really* fucking annoying. Why wouldn't it shut the hell up? That would never happen, so it wasn't worth thinking about.

However, the more I tried not to think about it, the harder it got to ignore it. To exact revenge for locking it in my mental box earlier, the fantasy from before once again overtook me. Safe in the privacy of the shower, it played out further in explicit detail. It left me no choice but to helplessly watch it unfold as my hand worked my erection.

Straddled on top of Rune, I rode him hard with a whimper. It overwhelmed me to feel him moving deep inside of me, filling me in a way I had never experienced before. I gasped, "I can't."

His hands glided up my thighs before sliding behind to cup my arse. "Yes, you can," he encouraged as he thrust into me. "Just let go. I've got you, baby."

My orgasm suddenly slammed into me with such force that I barely had time to cover my mouth to muffle my shout as I came hard. It caused my vision to blacken around the edges as my body shook from the intensity of my release. I sagged against the wall for support, shivering as the cold shower tiles shocked some sense into me.

Reality crashed into my high and yanked me down to the depths of despair. What the fuck was wrong with me? Why couldn't I be friends with someone without falling for them? I hadn't developed feelings for Felix or any of his acquaintances, so I assumed I had learned my lesson from Gregory. Yet, I couldn't stop having confusing feelings for Rune. How could I face him again, knowing I had gotten off to the thought of him being inside me? And why in God's name had I come from imagining him calling me *baby*?

Why couldn't I understand that this would end in nothing but disaster and heartache? Gregory had been my childhood best friend, and he violently rejected my interest when he learned about my years-long crush. I hadn't even known Rune two full weeks. How could I have such powerful feelings for him already?

Because he's smart, funny, kind, and the sexiest man to ever live. Your body came to life when he held your hand. Imagine what it would do if he did more than that.

With an agonized noise, I banged my head against the wall. It was bad enough to feel like that about him. Did I really need to torture myself, too?

What a shitty way to discover I was secretly a masochist.

I refused to let my stupid heart ruin another important friendship because it ignored the lesson from my last heartbreak. Rune was too amazing to lose, so I had to figure it out somehow. If I learned nothing else from Gregory, it was that silently suffering from unreturned feelings was infinitely preferable to losing a precious friend forever. I needed Rune in my life more than I wanted him to love me back.

Chapter Eight

RUNE

POPPING the collar of my red leather jacket against the cool night breeze, I kept my head down as I made my way to the Hurly-burly Bar and Grille near my apartment. I could have ordered in, but after my long flight back from Manhattan, I needed to stretch my legs and breathe in the fresh air as I walked. To avoid being recognized, I wore my thick, black glasses, even though people rarely bothered in my neighborhood.

My irritation over the New York photoshoot faded as I cleared my mind. Anytime Melissinda was involved, my stress skyrocketed. She was the woman I had filmed the elevator commercial with a few years ago. For some reason, she couldn't understand the difference between me being an excellent actor and being interested in her.

Melissinda had clung to me from the moment I first arrived. She was beautiful, but her passion for bedding famous guys was legendary at this point. Her ego was so large that she was incapable of comprehending that I wouldn't be attracted to her. In her mind, being gay was no excuse.

Even worse, Kevin had been there. He was a handsome stylist I had worked with several times before in the past who I hooked up with whenever I visited New York. Normally, I was all for enjoying an emotionless fuck with him. He was never clingy; he understood it was only about getting off and nothing more. Eager to please, he would do anything I asked. And god, that man sucked cock like a pro.

I hadn't had sex in almost a month after walking out on that pouty bottom whose name I couldn't remember for the life of me. It had been longer still since I had enjoyed a good fuck. I should have jumped at the chance to let Kevin satisfy me.

But as he flirted and touched me while getting me ready for the shoot, it had done nothing for me. I hadn't even been able to banter with him like normal because my heart wasn't in it. I had assumed it was from the stress of working with Melissinda. However, when Kevin invited me to go to his place, I blamed the jet lag for telling him no. It disappointed him, but he understood.

I didn't understand until he offered again on the second night why I turned him down. The thought of Callum's hurt expression haunted me. I knew it would devastate him if he found out I hooked up with

Kevin. The realization I was turning down Kevin for a virgin I wasn't going to fuck was absurd. I almost gave in to spite myself for being so stupid, but then I would think of Callum's pain and change my mind.

After missing out on enjoying all the pleasure Kevin's body offered, I expected to feel regret. Much to my surprise, staying alone in my hotel room and texting Callum all night was far more gratifying. He grew increasingly daring the more we talked. Most intriguingly, he was starting to flirt back.

I was playing with fire, and if I wasn't careful, it would end in disaster. Callum was an inexperienced virgin who was still idealistic enough to think sex was the same thing as making love. It would be impossible to fuck him without him falling in love with his whole heart. That was too much responsibility for me. When love factored into things, fucking got too messy and complicated. It was better to never let emotions ruin sex. Meaningless hookups with no strings attached were preferable to getting feelings involved. After all, you didn't need to fall in love to fuck.

Callum was too naïve for me to touch. His pure heart was something to be treasured by someone capable of loving him. He deserved better than my cynicism that scorned the very notion of love as being worthless and nonexistent.

I understood that, so why couldn't I stop wanting to show him what real pleasure was? A talentless virgin had nothing to offer me and didn't stand a chance of satisfying me. So, why did I want to play teacher and introduce him to the joys of sexual ecstasy? The only benefit to his virginity was he would be so impressionable that I could mold him into the lover I wanted. His eagerness to please and his boundless enthusiasm would translate in the bedroom once he got over his initial shyness and insecurity. Something told me he would be a *very* good student.

Everything about that appealed to the darkness within me, but it was wrong. It was *so* wrong. I was incapable of loving Callum the way he deserved, and I would be the world's biggest asshole for using him to satiate my temporary lust. As always, I'd get bored and move on once the thrill of the conquest was over, leaving him devastated and scarred for life. I liked him too much to do that to him.

The thoughts were too terrible to continue to entertain. He was coming over to my apartment tomorrow for dinner, and I would be a proper gentleman on my best behavior. I owed him that for being such a wonderful friend to me these last few weeks. Color had returned to my life because of him. My entire world was warmer and brighter thanks to him, and I refused to let my dumbass dick steal that from me.

Caught up in my thoughts, I almost walked right past the restaurant. I pushed aside my mental distraction as I entered and got in the line to order takeout. There were three people ahead of me, so I did a cursory scan around the mostly empty dining room to check if anyone recognized me. I did a double take when I spied Callum sitting at an enormous booth table near the back with four other guys. They looked a little older than him but seemed to be a tight-knit bunch.

I stepped out of line to indulge myself for a moment, enjoying watching him having a great time as he laughed with his friends. It gave me the same reviving sensation that a glass of ice-cold water did on the hottest day of the summer. I drank him in like a man dying of dehydration after being left out too long in the desert sands. His office had a casual-Friday policy, so it was my first time seeing him in jeans and a button-down black shirt. It was cute that even dressing down, he still wore a bow tie with green roses on it.

The mere sight of him loosened something in my chest I hadn't realized had even been tight. It became easier to breathe because he was nearby and happy. I yearned to go over there and make myself known, but it wasn't my place to intrude on him and his friends. Besides, I was there to grab a burger and head home to eat alone. He deserved his time with them.

Almost as if he felt me watching him, Callum turned and looked in my direction. Life became a movie where everything moved into slow motion when he saw me. Joy radiated from him as he beamed at me, drawing me to him. It had only been a week since I had last seen him, but I missed being in his sunny presence. The warmth and color he brought into my world exploded into technicolor now that I was near him again.

We stared at each other for a moment longer before he got up and came over to me. When he was close enough, he reached out to embrace me but stopped short. "Hi!"

"Hello, Callum." I loved greeting him by name because it always sent a visible shudder through him. It gratified me I affected him on that level. "If I didn't know any better, I would think you were about to hug me."

"Sorry, I was excited to see you here, and, um—well, I'm kind of a hugger, but if you're not, that's okay."

In truth, I was the furthest thing from a hugger. The only thing I liked less was cuddling. It was a physical form of emotion that I had never been comfortable with, which was why I never stuck around long after a hookup. The clinginess was cloying, not to mention deeply uncomfortable when I never reciprocated the emotions behind it.

But for some strange reason, I didn't want to turn him down. I was curious to find out what being hugged by him was like. My brother was the only person I never shoved off me. That was only because I had grown immune to his intense need for physical contact with those he loved. Plus, I had learned long ago that detangling from his hug was akin to wrestling a clingy octopus; you would always lose.

Unable to believe myself, I gestured to him in silent permission. Once again, his expression became one of pure happiness. He hugged me tightly like we were reuniting after being separated for a year instead of a week.

When I wrapped my arms around him, the din of the restaurant chatter and the entire world fell away. My existence became centered on the beautiful man I held. Rather than my normal desire to fetch a crowbar and pry off the offender, a peace unlike anything I had experienced before overcame me. My constant steam of anxieties quieted down for the first time in memory. He was short enough that I could rest my chin on his hair and smell the faintest trace of his shampoo. It was hard to place the exact scent, but it was something slightly sweet, exotic, and inviting.

I loved how he fit against me. He belonged right there, where I could hold him close and keep him safe from harm.

Nothing else mattered but the feeling of him pressed against me. It gave me an epiphany about what it meant to come home. It wasn't anything like going back to my empty apartment. This was a sense of returning to somewhere I belonged, where I was safe, loved, and wanted. He felt like *mine*—mine to hold, to protect, to love.

That thought should have terrified me, but the

devastating rightness kept me from panicking about it. I was too busy basking in the warm glow of unfamiliar contentment from a physical connection with someone. My brother's insistence on hugging had always baffled me, but if this was how he felt, I finally understood. Nothing bad could happen so long as Callum was with me.

His lips brushed against my neck, sending a shiver through me. My desire stirred from the tickle of his warm breath as he whimpered, "Oh, *god*, you smell *so good*."

I chuckled at his reaction. He stiffened, instinctively causing me to caress his hair to soothe him. It was something I had never done before, yet it was the most natural thing in the world to do with him. *Why?*

"Bollocks. I said that out loud, didn't I?" he whispered.

"Mm-hmm."

Callum groaned in embarrassment. "I'm sorry."

Without thought, I placed a gentle kiss against his forehead. "It's okay." I shouldn't have done that, but I didn't regret it. We set a record for my longest hug, but I still wasn't ready for it to be over yet. Part of me never wanted it to end.

He melted against me with a contented sigh. It thrilled me he didn't pull away and put distance between us. I didn't understand my willingness to continue holding him, but the satisfaction I derived from having him snuggled close was too immense to question.

When Callum leaned back far enough to gaze up at me with those beautiful dark blue eyes of his, my urge to draw him closer surprised me. With his flushed cheeks and parted lips, he was begging me to kiss him. It took an effort to fight my instincts not to lean down and give in to my desire. Oh, I was in serious trouble, wasn't I?

"Welcome back."

Once again, I had to restrain myself from doing the unforgivable. "It seems like you missed me."

He peered up at me through his long eyelashes. "I did."

"I missed you, too."

Callum stared up at me in disbelief. "You *did?*"

It was too late to deny it, so I ran with it instead. "I did. I'm glad I get to see you one day earlier."

With him so close, I absorbed the warm rays of his happiness like a cat basking in a sunny beam. I hadn't realized how much I missed that feeling only he gave me.

"Me, too. What are you doing here?" He asked that question with amazement, rather than accusation. I liked that.

"After I got home from the airport and took a shower, I didn't feel like cooking. This restaurant isn't that far from my apartment, and they have great burgers. I was about to get takeout when I saw you with your friends."

At the reminder of his witnesses, he tensed in my arms as a tiny *eep* escaped from him. It drove me to pull him closer and shield him. He glanced over his shoulder at them but didn't break free from our embrace. All four guys were gawking with grins. One waved, earning him an elbow from the man beside him.

Much to my pleasure, Callum once again hid his face against my chest. I rubbed his upper back to reassure him, pleased when he relaxed into my touch. He lingered for another moment, before he stepped away.

Why did I feel so empty without him near me? I'd have to figure out what the fuck was going on with my reaction later. When did I ever want to extend an already too long hug? *Since it felt so fucking good.*

Callum looked up at me with a resolved determination. It was adorable watching him straighten his bow tie as he built up his courage. "Would you, um, maybe like to join us? I mean, if you have plans, it's fine if you need to go. But if you don't, I would like it a lot—I mean, it would be nice if you would—but I don't want to impose or anything, so…"

Still suffering from the urge to touch him again, I reached out and squeezed Callum's shoulder in reassurance. I should have declined, gotten my burger to go, and gone home, but I wasn't ready to give him up yet.

However, meeting his friends put me at a dangerous risk of my identity being exposed. Then again, they would probably tell him who I was even if I left. He would have to learn who I was sometime, so it might as well be now while I was there to do any potential damage control. After taking a steadying breath and questioning my sanity, I agreed. "Sure."

To my great delight, he took my hand and led me over to the table. Once again, I loved the way his smaller one felt in mine as our fingers interlocked. Every part of him was made to fit me. I readied myself for meeting his buddies, which would be a first for me. I never stuck around long enough to learn a guy's last name, let alone meet people important to him.

When we reached the table, Callum released my hand as he introduced me. "Everyone, this is Rune." He gestured at the guy on his left. "This is Felix, who is Augie's younger brother."

"Hey, man. Nice to meet you," Felix said as we shook hands. He was a lanky, good-looking kid, with dark hair and striking gray-green eyes, wearing a faded T-shirt from a band I didn't recognize.

"Same."

Callum pointed at the guy closest to the wall on the opposite side of the booth. "That's North, Felix's roommate."

He was too far away to shake hands with, so I settled for a wave. "Hey."

North had wavy blond hair and hazel eyes, which blazed with lust as he blatantly checked me out from head to toe. "Damn, he wasn't joking. You're fucking *hot*."

Callum tensed up, and I resisted the urge to reach out and rest my hand on his lower back to calm him. Why did everything in me want to keep touching him? Instead, I smirked. "So I've been told."

"Ignore him, he's a perv," the guy next to him said, rolling his brown eyes over his friend's antics. He had on a yellow hoodie with a skull on it that wore a pink bow and had rainbow hearts for eyes. With his fuchsia spiky hair, it was quite the look. "Hi, I'm Wren. It's great to meet you."

I found it interesting that North offered no protests over being described in such a manner. "Likewise."

Wren put his hands on the shoulders of the guy sitting closest to me. "And this is Izzy, who is our resident smart-ass."

"You say that as if the rest of you are any different," he scoffed in a heavy French accent. With his fine features and high cheekbones, he could have been a model if he got connected with the right agent. The man projected European elegance with a regal bearing. There was something familiar about him, but I couldn't quite place why. He studied me with a slight frown that filled me with foreboding. "I know you."

"You know somebody this drop-dead sexy and didn't tell any of us?" North protested. "You dick!"

"Not personally." He narrowed his gaze as he struggled to discern who I was. My heart sank in my chest as I braced myself for him to reveal my identity. "You've lived in Paris before, *non?*"

That hadn't been the response I expected. Callum slid into the booth next to Felix and gestured for me to join him. I situated myself before answering, "Yeah, for a few years. How did you know?"

Izzy tapped his chin as his gaze travelled over my face. I saw the gears turning in his mind as he tried to figure out where he knew me from.

Before he guessed, our server came over to take our orders. I kept my head down as I ordered a burger, while the rest of them got dessert since they had eaten prior to my arrival.

After the server left, Izzy once again caught me by surprise. "You've worked with my brother. I remember your pictures."

"Dude, if there're pictures, you've gotta hook me up." North's comment earned him another elbow jab from Wren. "Ow! What did you do that for? I'm just saying! I mean, look at him!"

I ignored his outburst. "What's your brother's name?"

"Arsène Devereaux."

Oh, shit. Not only had I worked for Arsène as a model, but we had fucked for most of the time I lived in Paris. I had met him when I was an undergrad doing my study abroad program. Afterward, I reconnected with him when I moved back after graduating to advance my modeling career. It had been a few years since we had last met, but he was still at the top of the list of men I enjoyed. The odds of running into his younger brother were astronomical, but he was undeniably sitting in front of me. It felt like the cosmic universe was having a joke at my expense.

Put at risk of that part of my past being exposed to Callum, having him find out I was a professional model didn't seem as bad now. I cleared my throat as I refocused my attention. "Yeah, we worked together a few times when I lived there."

"What kind of work did you do for his brother?" Callum asked.

I attempted to downplay our personal relationship. "Back then, I had limited job options since I was there on a student visa. Modeling was one of the few ways I could make money under the table."

"You're being modest. He owes a lot of his career to you."

We had both boosted each other's profile in the fashion photography world, but I wasn't about to explain that in front of Callum. "Arsène did that through his own talent. A model isn't worth anything if the photographer doesn't know how to photograph him."

"Can we see the photos?" North asked.

Izzy gave him a pointed look that questioned, *Seriously?*

Callum fidgeted with his bow tie again. "Did you model for anyone else?"

Before I answered, Felix looked up from his phone. "Holy shit! You're that elevator guy, aren't you?"

And there it was. It was a miracle I had kept the secret from Callum for so long. I tried not to be bitter that I'd no longer have anonymity with him. It would be the ultimate test of trust to see if he was true to his word and didn't treat me any differently. "Yeah, that's me."

"Elevator guy?" God, Callum really had no idea. I would miss that.

Wren's jaw dropped at his friend's reaction. "Do you live under a rock? How have you not seen the elevator commercial? *Everyone's* seen it."

"Why would there be a commercial for elevators?" When the group laughed, Callum scowled. "I don't get it."

"The glasses threw me at first, but you have to know who he is now, right?"

"He's the younger brother of my boss's best friend." There was a wrinkle of distress in Callum's brow I wanted to smooth away. Bless him for being so earnest in his cluelessness.

"No, he's Rune *Tourneau*."

Even though I had prepared for it, I winced at my last name being exposed.

"You say that like it should mean something to me." The guys started laughing again, causing him to grow indignant. "It's not funny!"

"In Callum's defense, the glasses make him look different," Wren said.

"I never understood why people were dumb enough to believe Superman was Clark Kent because of a pair of glasses. Huh, I guess that shit works better than I thought," North added. "Either that, or we all got too distracted by your gorgeous face to have our brains make the connection at first."

Izzy tilted his nose in the air. "Speak for yourself. I knew exactly who he was."

"Well, I don't care who he is!" The show of backbone in my defense once again surprised me. There was something moving about seeing him overcome his shyness to stand up for me. Not to mention a little sexy. "He's just Rune to me, and he'll stay that way."

"But he's—ow!" North's knee hit the underside of the table as he jerked back from getting kicked, rattling the silverware. "Shit, that fucking hurt!"

"Oops, my foot must have slipped against your shin." Felix looked satisfied and unrepentant. "You're right, Callum. Sorry, Rune."

Our server brought our food, interrupting the conversation. I wasn't sure what to expect after she left, so I waited to see how everyone would react now that they were aware of who I was.

Felix was the first to speak. "Rune, if you could rewrite any fairy tale and make it gay, what would you choose?"

I had to applaud the kid for his off-the-wall topic starter. While I considered my answer, I ate a french fry. "I'd do *Cinderella* and call it *Cinderfella* instead."

"Ooh, that's a *fantastic* name!" Wren exclaimed.

"I'd go with *Snow White and the Seven Dwarves* and make it an all-out gay harem fuckfest," North declared. Everyone groaned over what I presumed was a predictable answer out of him. "What? It would be more fun than *Goldilocks and the Three Bears*. Big burly hairy bear guys aren't my thing."

"But tiny hairy ones are?" Izzy asked, setting off more laughter.

As we delved deeper into the subject of smutting up fairy tales, Callum glanced at me. The worry in his eyes over them outing my identity tugged at my heart.

I gave him a reassuring smile, my anxiety lifting when he returned it. The world had taught me to expect the worst, but I trusted things would be fine because it was him.

DESPITE THE ROUGH START, dinner ended up being fun. After the initial shock of my identity wore off, Callum's friends all treated me as if I was one of the guys. It had been a glimpse of what a normal life would be like, and it turned out I kind of enjoyed it.

Outside the restaurant, Felix, Izzy, North, and Wren stood off to the side to give Callum and me some privacy to say goodbye. Too bad they were doing a shit job of trying to act like they weren't watching us.

Callum had loosened up after he realized the revelation didn't upset me. However, the fear and worry returned to his beautiful blue eyes. It filled me with a need to make everything okay for him.

"I'm sorry they told me." His gaze pleaded with me for forgiveness.

"It's fine. I assumed that would happen when I agreed to meet them. Honestly, it went better than I expected."

"You have my word, I won't research you," Callum promised. "Nothing will change."

My arms ached with an unfamiliar desire for another hug. He was too precious for words. "I don't mind if you look me up online or watch the commercial. I believe you when you say it wouldn't change anything."

Apparently, he had the same urge, because he hesitated only a moment before hugging me again. The same as before, his snickering friends, the noisy traffic, the entire universe faded out. All that mattered was him. My residual stress dissipated as I relaxed from the comfort of his nearness. The experience was damn near euphoric.

"I don't care who you are. You're *my* Rune." He clung to me like the cutest koala bear in the world.

His Rune? It was a thought I should rebel against, because I belonged to no one but me. And yet…I didn't hate it? I liked the Rune that I was around him, because that was the real me that I could only be with him. That Rune had room in his heart for Callum and wanted to cherish him for the gift that he was. That Rune was who I wished I was all the time.

"Uh, I mean, not that you're *mine*, but—"

I shushed his rambling and held him tighter. Why did stroking his soft hair bring me so much peace? What was it about holding him that completed me in a way I hadn't thought was possible before? Everything was right in my world when he was in my embrace, and I never wanted to let him go.

After this, I owed my brother an apology for criticizing his need to hug people. Holding Callum was more satisfying than sex in a lot of ways, and I didn't know what to make of that. Sex left me hollow and unfulfilled, but hugging him restored me with an addicting satisfaction.

Callum breathed in deep again to smell my cologne. He moaned with pleasure, causing my dick to stir with interest. It seemed to do the same for him, because he grew erect against me. I experienced an intense need to say screw decency and take him home with me. There was so much I could teach him…

When he jerked away, I longed to bring him back into my arms. It was such a strange urge that I couldn't act on it. Instead, I gave him the courtesy of pretending not to notice, even though the bastard in me wanted to take advantage of his arousal. "Does coming over tomorrow at six for dinner work for you?"

He straightened his already straight bow tie while working up the nerve to say something. "Could I…"

"You can do anything you want, Callum. All you have to do is ask."

He took a deep breath before requesting, "Could I—um, that is, if it's not a problem—could I maybe come over a little earlier to watch you cook? I really want to watch. But only if that's okay with you. And if it isn't weird. Is it weird? It's probably weird. I'm so sorry."

It was cute how he worried his lower lip with his teeth when he was nervous. "It's not weird. Let's make it five o'clock, then."

He brightened with excitement, which toyed with my heartstrings. It took so little for him to be happy. His delighted smile was worth agreeing to damn near anything. "Thanks for tonight. I hope you had a good time."

"Any time with you is a good time." I meant the

words with a sincerity that surprised me. "Good night, Callum."

As he trembled from me saying his name, it was too much temptation to resist. I leaned down and pressed a soft kiss on each of his smooth cheeks. His dumbstruck disbelief made me want to claim his lips next, but I refused to do that on a public street in the presence of his friends. He wasn't mine to enjoy. That was a pleasure for another man someday. The guy didn't even exist yet, and I already hated the bastard who would never be worthy of Callum's love.

I couldn't resist teasing him. "What? It's been a while since I've lived in Europe, but I thought all Europeans kissed like that."

It was my turn to be the shocked one when he returned the favor. He braced his hand against my chest and went up on tiptoe to kiss each of my cheeks. His actions sent a hot flare of lust through me I was unprepared for, leaving me ravenous for something other than food.

"I'll see you tomorrow, Rune. Night!"

With those words, he rushed over to his friends, who all started making a fuss about what he had done as they walked away. I stared at them dumbfounded and wondered how the hell sweet, innocent, virginal Callum had turned the tables on me so fast.

Shit, I'm in so *much trouble.*

Chapter Nine

CALLUM

OH, I was *fucked*. Not just a little fucked, but well and truly fucked. And it was all my fault.

In my excitement at unexpectedly seeing Rune, I had almost hugged him. While I had the foresight to stop short, when he offered me an invitation, I couldn't refuse.

When he wrapped his arms around me, I blew past the "resisting my growing feelings for him" stage and lost my whole damn heart to him. The love and comfort I found in his embrace had pushed me over that edge into free-falling. I felt so close to him, forgetting the world and people existed. Curled up against him, I ached to crawl into his soul and become one with him. In that single perfect moment, I had everything I ever wanted.

God, and the *smell* of him. I wished I could drown in him and never come back up for air. It made me want to taste him. I didn't know enough about cologne to tell what the individual notes were, but he smelled comforting and masculine. It gave me the strangest sense of having finally found my heart's home, while also stoking the burning fires of lust inside of me. The simultaneous urge to cuddle him forever and have him throw me down on the bed to have his wicked way with me confused me.

He had indulged my clinging to him, and I had repaid by getting hard because he smelled so fucking *good*. If there was any fairness in this world, I prayed he hadn't noticed before I stepped out of his arms. That had been almost impossible to do while my hormones begged me to climb him like a tree.

And I had called him *my* Rune. Talk about cringe. I had no right to claim him. He was my friend, but he wasn't *my* Rune. He would never be that. But when he held me as if I was what he treasured most, how could I not feel that way? I longed for him to be mine because my heart was already his, whether he wanted it or not. Who was I kidding? He wouldn't want it. That would only be a burden to him.

After my friends revealed Rune's identity, I was lucky he had let me hug him a second time. I thought for sure that he would be upset and standoffish afterward, but he had comforted me about it. It piqued my curiosity why the guys had been so hung up on the elevator thing, but it would be a betrayal to find out. Rune deserved better.

My head was still a mess when I got home. I wanted to slip into my room unnoticed, but Brody and Augie were curled up on the couch together watching a cooking show. It tugged at my heart because I now understood to some extent what that felt like, and I wanted more of it.

Brody paused it and gestured for me to come over to them. "How was dinner?"

"It was fine." In some ways, it was the best night ever. But it also devastated me to have a glimpse of what I was missing.

Augie looked at me with concern. "Are you sure about that?"

"No." I undid my bow tie with a discouraged sigh.

He sat up straight with a worried expression. "What happened?"

I got a taste of bliss, and I'm a greedy bastard who wants more than I can have. How could I explain my mess? I did the next best thing instead. "Do you know who Rune Tourneau is?"

"Why? Have you been looking at my browser history or something?" my brother joked.

His reaction threw me for a loop. "Is he in there?"

Augie snorted. "He's probably in both of ours, let's be honest."

The thought that they both had looked him up before made an unpleasant jealousy curdle in the pit of my stomach.

Brody smirked at his boyfriend. "Let me guess—elevator commercial?"

"Guilty."

The answer only made him grin more. "Same."

I threw up my hands with an exasperated sigh. "What's so special about a stupid elevator commercial? I don't get it!"

They burst out laughing at my question, causing me to huff in annoyance. Why was that *everyone's* reaction?

Augie got control of himself first. "Oh, do yourself a favor and go watch it. You'll understand why after that."

Frustrated, I clenched my hands into fists at my side. "I don't want to!"

"What's going on, Cally?"

My irritation grew as I explained, "I'm apparently the only person who doesn't know who Rune Tourneau is."

"You might not know his name, but you'd know him if you saw him," Augie said. "He's a model who has been in a ton of famous ads. The elevator ad is what he's most known for since it went viral a few years ago."

"I read books, which don't have ads in them," I defended myself. "I usually don't watch TV, and if we do, we fast-forward through the commercials. Plus, if it was a while ago, I was still in Ireland and wouldn't have seen an American commercial. How famous can a guy be if he's advertising elevators, anyway?"

"No, it isn't an ad for them. It's a cologne ad that takes place in one."

I threw up my arms in frustration. "That makes even less sense! How does that sell a fragrance?"

"You should see for yourself rather than have someone tell you," Brody told me. "It's more fun that way."

I battled against myself as I stared at the floor. While I didn't want to betray Rune's trust, I also hated being the only ignorant one. My resolve to do the right thing slipped away at an alarming rate. I had already violated our friendship once tonight by getting aroused while hugging him, and there I was, contemplating doing another unthinkable thing. Worst of all, I had fallen for another friend I could never have after swearing I wouldn't do that again. Why was I so bad at life?

Brody came over and gathered me up into a tight bear hug. It was a different comfort from Rune's, but it shattered my tenuous grip on my emotions. I felt three centimeters tall as I sobbed against his muscular chest. My brother was patient as I cried about more than a stupid commercial. Why did love always hurt so much?

When I quieted down to tiny sniffles, Brody asked, "What are you really upset about?"

"I want to watch, but I *can't*," I mumbled against his poor shirt. I had made a mess all over it.

"Why not?"

My voice cracked in my grief. "It's too risky. I promised him nothing would change, but what if it does?"

"Him? Wait, are you telling me that the Rune you've been seeing these past few weeks is Rune *Tourneau*?"

I avoided his gaze. "Apparently. We ran into him at dinner tonight, and the guys all knew who he was, and I didn't."

"Jesus, Mary, and Joseph. No wonder you're all mixed-up inside."

"I like *my* Rune." Damn it, I needed to quit calling him that, but it was true. "I don't want to be the same as everyone else in his life."

Brody led me over to sit on the couch between him and Augie. I used a tissue from the side table, but it didn't help at all.

"Seeing him in an ad won't change how you treat him. That's not who you are."

"But he liked that I didn't know who he was." I sighed with another stuffed-up sniff. "He said I could look him up, but that would make me the worst friend in the world."

"If he told you he was okay with it, then take him at his word," Augie said. "Not knowing is more likely to drive a wedge between you two."

I furrowed my brow in confusion. "What do you mean?"

"Being Rune Tourneau is who he is. If you reject that by not learning about him, that means there will always be a part of him you won't accept."

My brother nodded in agreement. "He's right. Rune can never be completely himself if you refuse to acknowledge the Tourneau side of him now that you know. That would hurt your relation—your friendship."

I took a moment to process their words. "So, you're saying by *not* watching, I'm being a worse friend than if I did?"

"You're a wonderful friend no matter what, but yeah." Brody patted my shoulder. "From everything you've said, he seems like a straightforward guy. If he gave you permission, then he wants you to know. And you don't have to worry when you bring him over here. We won't treat him any differently. He's still your Rune to us, okay?"

A weight lifted off my chest when he hugged me again. After that, I embraced Augie in gratitude for his excellent advice. "Thank you. I think I'll get some sleep. See you in the morning."

After we exchanged good-nights, I headed upstairs to my room and locked the door. What they had said made sense, so I felt a lot better about what I was about to do.

I sat down at my desk, then pulled up a browser

on my laptop and typed in *Rune Tourno*. The search engine responded with *Showing results for Rune Tourneau.* Great, I couldn't even spell his bloody name right.

His headshot and information popped up in the sidebar. The first link was his social media page, followed by his modeling agency profile. I clicked on that for his portfolio.

It opened to a black-and-white shot of him laying naked in bed, with the sheet strategically placed for modesty. He had a lithe frame, but his muscles were chiseled perfection to die for. With his fingers embedded in his tousled hair, the pose gave the impression of him being freshly fucked. He gazed at the camera with alluring bedroom eyes, inviting me to join him for round two. I swallowed hard, struggling against my powerful surge of hormones. Maybe this wasn't such a good idea.

I advanced to the second image. Rune wore a Gio Zapfirino tuxedo and bow tie, looking like the sexiest James Bond cosplayer of all time as he straightened his cuffs. He was cool, confident, and ready to seduce. My heart beat out of my chest as I fought against my arousal. Fuck, no one should look that good in clothes. It should have been impossible.

Yet again, I appreciated Jules's foresight in not telling me who his younger brother was before I met him in the café. Rune was so attractive in his photos that I never in a million years would have had the confidence to meet him in person. I barely survived as it was. But now that he was in my life, I couldn't imagine it without him.

Once I gathered my resolve, I clicked for the next picture. It showed Rune embracing a stunning woman from behind, his beautiful hands roaming her body as he made eye contact with the camera. His lips were just about to brush against her neck as she writhed in ecstasy against him.

It was impossible to stop myself from imagining him flush against me, his fingers trailing over my skin as he kissed up to my ear. Heat pooled in my belly, and tendrils of lust snaked through me, tempting me to act out on my forbidden desires.

With a distressed noise, I closed the website tab. That was too hot to handle, and I didn't stand a chance of browsing the entire portfolio without losing control of my desire.

To distract myself, I got ready for bed. After I finished changing and came back from the bathroom, I had settled down. It wasn't like it was news to me that Rune was a walking sex god. I may make a donkey's arse out of myself with him sometimes, but I could still carry on a conversation with him. Even though I had seen a few sexy pictures, everything would be fine.

Confident I could withstand more, I sat in front of my computer again. Three videos came up on the search results. The first was the cologne ad, the second was a profile on him, and the third was an interview. I squinted at the small preview picture showing him alone in an elevator. Nothing about that image explained everyone's reactions, so I plugged in my headphones and clicked on it to see what all the fuss was about.

It started with the doors sliding open, revealing Rune standing in the center. He looked fine as hell in his suit and red tie. A woman in a little black dress and high heels walked into the frame with a sway of her hips. She pressed herself against him, leaning in close to sniff his neck, then ran her tongue up it toward his ear with a sensual moan. I covered my mouth to smother the squeak that escaped from me as she did what I had fantasized about doing earlier tonight.

She reached out and yanked his tie to pull him closer. He reacted by pressing her hard against the elevator wall and ravaging her pouty lips as he pinned her in place. I could hear the erotic sounds of their heavy breathing and slick wetness of their kiss. The passion was aggressive, animalistic, and I couldn't look away.

He hitched one of her legs up toward his hip, allowing him to run his hand up the garter belt on her pale thigh, before groping her ass. When she wrapped her other leg around him, he hoisted her against the wall and thrust against her like he was fucking her. She cried out as he moaned, and then there was a disorienting quick cut. They were now standing side by side in the middle of the elevator, straightening their clothing back to decency. She walked out with a longing backward glance. He inclined his head and stroked his neck with a smirk and cocky chuckle, winking at her before the doors slid closed again. The brand logo and cologne bottle appeared, but I barely noticed.

Fuckfuckfuckfuckfuckingfuck!

That was the only word I had to react to what I had just seen. It was one thing to imagine what being with Rune would be like in my mind, but seeing him mimicking fucking someone was too much. I quivered as the hellfire flames of lust licked at me, leaving me desperate for Rune's touch. I ached with an unfamiliar need for him to dominate me in the same manner. My breathing came out in heavy pants as if he had ravished me in the elevator instead of her.

It urged me to commit a heinous sin as I crawled out of my skin with a mad desire unlike anything I had experienced before. The rational part of my brain told me I should take a cold shower and stop thinking about the commercial, but my need was too strong. It filled me with so much wanting that it hurt. The only way to make that ache disappear was to satiate it.

Like a man possessed, my body reacted on autopilot as I slid my underwear and green flannel pajama pants down enough for my prick to spring free. The tip of it was already glistening with a hint of my arousal. Despite the uncomfortable sense of wrongness, I restarted the video from the beginning.

At the sight of Rune, I tightly gripped my cock. I bit my lower lip to hold in my reactions as I worked my hardness to memories of how good he smelled. When he caged her against the wall, a strangled whimper escaped me as I imagined him pinning me instead. My hand picked up speed as he groped her arse and thrust like they were really having sex. I was so close, so painfully close as they straightened their clothes after they finished.

When Rune caressed his own neck with an arrogant chuckle, my toes curled as I tensed. I teetered right on the edge, finally pushed over by his flirty wink. I almost didn't have enough time to cover my mouth with my other hand before exploding all over myself in spurts with a muffled cry.

Like last week in the shower, my orgasm plowed into me so hard that I forgot how to function. Everything went offline from the surging overload. I didn't even have the wherewithal to be embarrassed by my fast finish.

As I came down from my high, the physical relief was immense. However, the guilt ruined my euphoria as I glared down at my hand covered in the evidence of my betrayal. I was no better than everyone else who got off on how sexy he was. How was I supposed to see him tomorrow, knowing what I did tonight? He may have told me I could watch, but he damn well didn't give me permission to have a wank at his expense.

Tears welled up in my eyes as I slammed my laptop monitor lid closed with my clean hand in disgust. How could I let Rune down when he trusted me? I didn't deserve him or his trust.

With a heavy heart, I cleaned myself up before crawling into bed and curling up into a miserable ball under the covers. I allowed myself one more sin for the night and fell asleep remembering the pleasure of being held in his embrace.

Chapter Ten

RUNE

"YOU LOOK like you want to ask me something but don't know how to say it." My brother grinned as he sat beside me on my living room couch.

Jules was right, because he always was. Since embracing Callum the previous evening, I had been trying to solve the mystery of why it made me feel so good. Despite my best efforts, I still hadn't found the answer I was searching for yet.

"You know you can ask me anything."

It was true. My older brother was the most open and honest person I had ever met in my life. It was embarrassing to admit my problem out loud, though. I eased into the awkward conversation. "Why do you like hugs?"

"Because they're the best."

"How?"

"It varies based on who and under what circumstances. Hugging someone to comfort them, being embraced by somebody you love versus a friend, all of those are distinct experiences. But they're great for varying reasons."

I heaved an agitated sigh. Why did it have to be so fucking complicated?

My brother studied me. "Why are you suddenly so interested in something you hate?"

"Because hugs always feel like someone is forcing their emotions onto me. It obligates me to accept and reciprocate something I'm incapable of feeling." My skin crawled with discomfort at the thought. "They're unpleasant and claustrophobic. I've always hated them, even as a kid. You know that."

"Too bad running away screaming 'no' doesn't work as well when you're an adult," Jules teased. "I know I'm lucky you tolerate me doing it."

"You're my brother and I love you. It's important enough to you that I can put up with it for a few seconds."

"Is this your passive-aggressive way of telling me to stop doing that?"

I shook my head. "No, I'm just trying to figure it out."

"Figure out what?"

Why does hugging Callum feel like the best thing ever? It's how I wanted to answer, but I couldn't put it into words. It embarrassed me to admit not only had it felt incredible, but I ached to hug him the instant he walked into my apartment later that evening.

Realization dawned in my brother's eyes. "*Ohhhhh.* I see."

"Huh?"

"Callum hugged you and you didn't hate it."

His insight stunned me. "How the hell could you possibly know that?"

"What else would make you question your stance on hugging if not him? Or is it not just you didn't hate it—you *liked* it?"

There weren't enough words for the level of pleasure I had derived from holding Callum in my arms. How did I explain why something I hated was suddenly life changing? "It felt…"

After I trailed off, Jules encouraged me. "Say it."

"It felt…*good*. Amazing, even. All my anxiety disappeared, and I was *complete*. It was like coming home. I don't understand why I didn't want to let him go."

"See? I told you, it's the best feeling of all time." He smiled at me with pride. "What you described is how it feels for me."

"With everyone?"

He shook his head. "No, only with someone you're in love with, who has all of your heart."

"I am *not* in love with him!" The idea was preposterous. "I don't *do* love."

"Sure you don't." I resented his amused snort.

"What other reason would there be for why hugging him is more satisfying than sex with strangers? Why else can't you wait to hold him again the next time you see him? What other explanation is there for why you can be your real self with him that you can't share with anybody but him?"

His words hit me hard, but I still protested. "That's impossible. He's just a naïve kid who—" I stopped myself from finishing my sentence. I couldn't say he was just a naïve kid who didn't matter, because he *did* matter to me. Deeply. Against all the odds, he had brought vibrancy back into my life. I was living again because of him and not just going through the motions. "Callum believes in true love. He deserves somebody who can give that to him. That person isn't me."

"You would really be okay with him being with some other guy?"

Callum being with another man made my stomach churn with burning acid. He was too inexperienced to know which men to avoid. The prospect of some bastard hurting him filled me with an incandescent rage. They would destroy his innocence and faith in romance, leaving him battered and broken. It was unbearable. He wasn't mine to protect, but that urge blazed inside of me all the same.

My brother couldn't hide his smile. "That guy doesn't exist, and you already want to beat the shit out of him for what he hasn't done to Callum yet."

"He's too sweet and trusting. They'll take advantage of him!"

Jules's smile turned into a full grin. "You want to protect him, don't you?"

"Of course I do! He deserves better than being abused by men who only think with their dicks."

My brother continued. "You want to wrap him up in your embrace and keep him safe from anyone who would try to harm him. Because the thought of someone breaking his heart makes your own feel like shattering."

The mere possibility of that happening crushed mine in a vise. I clutched at my chest, finding it harder to breathe. Why was Callum's devastation so agonizing to me? What was it about him that triggered my instinctive urge to do anything necessary to put a smile on his face?

"Thinking of him being in pain hurts, doesn't it?" Jules asked. "You'd move Heaven and Earth if that's what would make him happy. You won't feel better until he's back with you again."

It didn't make sense to me. "Why do I feel like that?"

"Because that's what being in love is, Rune. The only way to stop other men from hurting him is if he's with you."

"But I'm too cynical, and—"

He cut me off. "If you were too cynical, you wouldn't be able to see the good in him at all, nor would you care. You would fuck him and leave him without a second thought. Instead, you're sitting over there in agony over someone hypothetically hurting him and ruining his optimistic outlook on life. People who are too cynical don't have that reaction."

I opened my mouth to argue, but the words wouldn't come out. The best I could muster up was, "He should be treasured."

"By who? Who would be good enough to be with him?"

Once again, his question rendered me mute. Callum being with someone else burned me with a jealousy I had no right to feel. "Goddamn it, he's not mine!"

"But you want him to be."

"Yes, but I don't deserve him!" My eyes went wide in shock at my declaration. I hadn't realized I felt that way.

Jules refused to accept my bullshit. "Why the fuck not? What have you done that makes you so unworthy?"

"He's too good for me," I snarled. "I'm one of those immoral men who would use him for my own sexual amusement and dump him the second I tired of him." That was how I had treated every other man in my life, because meaningless hookups were all I was prepared to handle. I wasn't equipped for love.

"Do you *really* think you'd get bored with Callum?"

He was too full of surprises for that. It forced me to argue a different angle. "I'm a slip out in the middle of the night type of asshole. He needs someone to cuddle him in the morning and make him chocolate chip pancakes with whipped cream for breakfast." I bristled when Jules laughed. "What's so fucking funny?"

"You don't find that an oddly specific example of what Callum needs?" He continued snickering at me. "Because that sure sounds like something you want to do for him versus some other random guy."

I could picture that kind of morning clearly in my mind. It aroused me imagining him standing in my kitchen, wearing only my shirt from the night while he watched me cook. The white button-down would be far too big on him, showing off one of his pale shoulders as it slipped to the side. I loved thinking of him cooing as he ate my delicious breakfast. The only thing better would the taste of sweet chocolate chip pancakes on his lips as I kissed him afterward and carried him backward to bed. The vision suffused me with that same warm fuzzy feeling of peace and contentment that hugging Callum did. *Why?*

"That. That right there," Jules said, interrupting my reverie. "What you just thought about, that's love."

"It's…" I tried to protest, but I couldn't say it. Because it did feel like love, and for the first time, it was something I wanted, even if I didn't deserve it.

"Imagine your life without whatever you were thinking about."

There was no point in imagining it, because that's how I had lived until I met Callum. I remembered all those nights I had snuck out of some nameless stranger's bed while they slept. I always returned to my empty apartment and for a small breakfast to eat alone as I wallowed in my misery. Callum had filled that aching void inside me, taking away years of painful shadows with the brightness of his sunshine.

"Now do you understand? You're allowed to want love, Rune. You're allowed to want *him*."

"But he's a kid." It was an actual concern, but I smiled as I remembered his text from before: *I'm a virgin, not a minor, thank you very much.*

"Yes, but one who is very mature for his age. And as emotionally stunted as you are, it evens the playing field between you when you think about it. Plus, you're technically both virgins, so quit worrying."

I laughed at the ridiculous notion. "How am I a virgin when I've been fucking around for over a decade?"

"Yes, you traded in your V-card for having sex a long time ago, but you just had your cherry popped discovering satisfying hugs with him. You're still a love virgin."

"A *love virgin*?" I arched my eyebrows. "What the hell is that?"

"You've never been in love until you met him. Sure, you have plenty of experience fucking without feelings to get off. But you haven't made love before. You're just as inexperienced as him in that area. The two of you'll fumble around a bit as you try to figure out how to make it work, but your relationship will be stronger for it."

Well, shit. He had a point. "I don't even know if I'm capable of that, though. Sex has always been sex."

"Yes, because your heart has never gotten involved. Think about how good it feels when Callum hugs you. Now, imagine how much better it'll be when he embraces you with his whole body and heart. *That's* what making love is like."

I couldn't fathom that level of connection with another person. But if anyone could make me feel that way, it was Callum. There were other concerns, though. "Everyone'll assume I'm some kind of predator for going after such a young guy."

Jules rolled his eyes. "Since when did you care what people think about you?"

"The optics aren't great."

"Fuck the optics," he said with a dismissive wave. "Yeah, there'll be assholes talking shit about him being your boy toy, but who cares? None of that matters when you're happy with him."

"Is this why you introduced us? Because you knew I'd fall for him?"

He grinned at my question. "It may or may not have been on my list of differentials for outcomes."

"I can't be angry with you for it when he's the best thing that's ever happened to me. But what if he doesn't—"

Jules held up his hand to stop me. "Don't say something that stupid. I noticed how he looked at you when we were in the office. I also may have heard from two little birds all about how cute you both were at your six-hour lunch. That kid is head over heels in love with you, Rune. It's your job to make sure he knows that's okay."

It wasn't surprising that Renée and Maria had talked to my brother. I could at least take solace in how much they loved to give Jules shit for not being honest with Xander about his feelings.

There was something else bothering me. "Callum fell for his friend before, and it ended badly. What if he's so hung up on that baggage that he won't be open to being with me?"

"I'm sure you can explain the difference between an older gay man who desires him versus a young straight boy who isn't interested," Jules retorted. "He has more reasons to believe you could never want him, so you have to let him know how you feel. Don't leave any doubt in his mind about your commitment to loving him with all that you are."

"That's what Renée said."

"When she's right, she's right." He shrugged, then

got the conversation back on track. "Remember to be patient with him. Before he gets scared off, you need to convince him the famous Rune Tourneau who could have anyone in the world really wants him. Don't hold his disbelief against him. Reassure him as often as it takes without getting frustrated."

It was solid advice, but I was unaccustomed to expressing myself, let alone repeatedly. "Use my words. Got it."

"Good. I should go so you can get ready for tonight." Jules stood up, and I escorted him over to the door. "Oh, and one more thing."

"Yes?"

"Don't rush. You're used to jumping straight into sex. He probably hasn't had his first kiss yet. Give him time to process that experience before you overwhelm him with what comes next. You don't have to get all your firsts over with in one go."

I nodded. "That makes sense."

"Rune, I mean it. Savor the small moments instead of aiming for instant gratification. If he gets overwhelmed, slow down further. Listen to what he needs, and don't decide for him because you have all the know-how. Everything will be different with him, so your previous experience of wham, bam, thank you, and goodbye won't count for jack shit with him. Go at his speed, even if you're dying from the glacial pace."

I hesitated before hugging my brother. He made a

surprised noise but returned the embrace. I could feel the brotherly love Jules always offered me without fail, despite me being a stubborn ass about accepting that sometimes. "Thank you."

He squeezed me tighter, but for once, I found it comforting rather than constricting. "You deserve this, no matter what your inner demons tell you. You've got this. Tell me how it goes."

"I will."

He beamed at me with joy. "I'm really happy for you, Rune. Love you, and I'll talk to you later."

"Thanks, love you, too." I waved as he left.

Jules had given me a lot to think about, but he was right. It was time for me to act my age and stop listening to my doubts. Callum was worth the effort. I'd do anything so I could have the chance to make him breakfast someday and see his smile.

BY THE TIME five o'clock rolled around, I had an unusual jittery sense of anticipation. I had tried to plan for when to talk to Callum about everything and decided it would be best to wait until after dinner was over. Unfortunately, all those plans went right out the window when I opened my door and saw him standing there on the verge of tears. Appreciating how cute he looked in his black suit, white shirt, and rainbow ombre bow tie decked out with glitter would have to wait until he was in a better state of mind.

He stepped closer to hug me, then shied away as if he thought better of it. Being denied was shockingly painful and made me realize how much I had been looking forward to it. However, I didn't take it personally given how upset he was. I ushered him into my living room to sit on my couch. "What's wrong?"

Callum's dark blue eyes filled with despair, pleading with me to understand. Everything in me wanted to pull him into my lap and make the hurt stop, but I resisted the urge until I knew what was going on with him.

"You can tell me."

He glanced away in shame. "I'm the worst. I shouldn't be here."

The words were distressing to hear, but I focused on reassuring him. "None of that is true. You're not, and I want you here more than anything."

Tears welled up in his eyes. "You wouldn't if you knew what I did yesterday."

It wasn't hard to connect the dots after that. "Callum, I meant it when I said you could look me up online. It doesn't bother me at all, so please don't let it ruin your evening."

"I didn't want to, because you liked that I didn't know." He continued fighting back tears. "But I was afraid you'd think I rejected the Tourneau part of you, which meant I had to do it to be a good friend."

It moved me to hear how deeply he had mulled over the issue. I didn't get why that upset him, though. "You're the best friend I've ever had."

"No, I'm not."

To comfort him, I reached out and caressed his cheek. "I promise you are."

He nuzzled against my hand before he jerked back. "I don't deserve you."

It stunned me to hear my own words I had said to my brother echoed back to me now. Jules had been correct; Callum needed explicit reassurance. "Yes, you do. You're all that is good and right with this world. You deserve everything and then some."

A sob escaped him, but he held his tears at bay. "Not after last night." His gaze drifted to my throat and lingered there for a moment before he glanced away again.

I had an inkling about what might have happened, but I wasn't sure. To test my theory, I said his name to get him to look at me, then caressed my neck. "What did you do?"

He stared, transfixed, before hiding his face in his hands. "I'm so sorry!"

His reaction confirmed my suspicions. I kept my tone neutral as I asked, "Did you watch my commercial?"

Callum curled up on himself with an agonized noise, guilt and shame radiating off him in waves.

"I told you I was fine with you seeing it. I'm not

upset with you for doing that. There's no reason for you to beat yourself up like this."

He mumbled something into his hands, but I didn't catch it.

"What?"

"I didn't just watch it."

Well, *that* was an interesting admission. I wasn't oblivious to the fact that the sexy nature of the ad was what caused it to go viral. Rather than disgust me, him getting off on it was an enormous turn-on. "Callum, did you touch yourself while watching me?"

He shuddered at my seductive tone. When he tried to leave, I captured his hand and tugged him back onto my couch. I stroked the inside of his wrist with my thumb, raising chills on his pale skin. "Did you come because of me?"

A tear finally fell down his cheek. "Yes."

I leaned closer and kissed it away. He stiffened under me with a confused noise but didn't try to leave again. My ego rumbled with contentment. "Good."

"Good?"

His innocent reaction made me want to cuddle him forever. "*Very* good."

"Why?"

Unable to resist the urge any longer, I guided him onto my lap. It felt like my missing piece had slid into place, finally completing me. "I enjoy giving you pleasure."

"B-b-but I betrayed our friendship! You should be mad at me!"

"My sole regret is I wasn't there."

He shifted position to stare at me in disbelief. "*What?*"

It was hard to hold back my smirk. "I said, my sole regret is I wasn't there. I would have loved to help."

"*Help?*"

"Mm-hmm." I caressed his flushed cheek. God, I loved touching him so much.

"What do you mean, *help*? Help me *what*?"

It was too enjoyable to answer, "Help you come."

His mouth dropped open as several interrupted syllables fell out of him, but he couldn't string together a sentence to save his life. It was adorable.

I traced the outline of his jaw, marveling at his soft skin. "Would that please you?"

More broken sounds escaped from him as he stared at me.

"It would please me. Very much, actually." Talk about vast understatements. Nothing would bring me greater joy than pleasuring him.

Words were still beyond him, so he settled for a frustrated noise of confusion.

My brother's comments about knowing when to ease off for Callum's sake came back to me, so I quit teasing him for now. I guided him to meet my gaze. "Listen, I'm not mad at you for doing that. Don't feel guilty or upset or worried that you betrayed me or our friendship because my commercial aroused you. You're not in trouble, and we're still friends, okay? Trust me, I'm more than fine with it."

It was a physical relief when his distress subsided at my words, but he seemed lost. "But what I did should disgust you!"

"Why?"

"Because it was wrong. You're my friend, so I shouldn't have—"

I shushed his fears. "Stop right there. You have my explicit permission to get off to thoughts of me as often as you want. In fact, I encourage it."

He startled backward in shock. It took him several failed attempts before he could ask, "You *want* me to wank off to you?"

"That's *exactly* what I'm saying."

"I don't—why would you—*what?*"

Unaccustomed to being open with someone, my stomach was in knots with anxiety, but I made myself tell the truth. "I don't only want to be friends, Callum. I want to love you and show you what real pleasure is. That's why you getting off while thinking about me is so exciting."

To my surprise, Callum's reaction was to pinch his arm until he exclaimed, "Ow!"

"What are you doing?"

He did it a second time before staring at me with a consternated look. "I wanted to check if this was a dream, because there's no way in real life you would ever want to love someone like me."

"You're right. I don't want to love someone *like* you," I told him. "I love *you*."

"You love me?" he asked in a small voice. "Like love-me-like-a-boyfriend love me? For real?"

It amazed me how easy it was to answer that question. "If that's what you want."

"*Of course* that's what I want, but I'm not allowed—"

I pressed a finger against his lush lips. "Yes, you are. It would make me the happiest man on the planet if you felt the same about me, too."

"But you could have *anyone*," he protested. "Why would you settle for an inexperienced virgin who has no clue about what he's doing?"

"Because you read books for me and laugh when I send you eighteenth-century dick pics. You share my passion for history and know about the Plantagenets. I like who I am with you, because that's the real me that I had almost forgotten existed. I want to cook for you and treasure you for the gift you are. And you're by far the cutest person I've ever met."

He threw his arms around me and buried his face against my shoulder. "I love you, too, but I didn't think you'd be interested in me."

My heart soared at hearing he reciprocated my feelings. "I'm not like your idiot friend. Unlike him, I understand how precious you are. Don't worry about whether you're worthy of Rune Tourneau. He doesn't matter. I'm *your* Rune who loves only you. You *never* have to doubt that. But if you do, I'll tell you as many times as you need to hear it to know how much I love you. I don't want to just be your first boyfriend. I want to be your only one ever."

Callum's open joy and adoration made my soul sing with happiness. To my delight, he leaned forward and gave me a lingering, chaste kiss. It set off an explosion of pleasure in me as I basked in the sweetness. I would have expected him to be shy and need coaxed, but I loved that he always surprised me.

"Was that okay? That was my first time, so…"

"It was perfect." I reassured him by pulling him closer and kissing him again. His stomach grumbling a complaint interrupted us. I chuckled at his sheepish expression. "Come on, let's go start dinner."

As we walked to the kitchen, he took my hand in his and interlaced our fingers. That small action launched a fireworks finale inside me, showering down sparks of happiness and contentment as I cooked.

Chapter Eleven

CALLUM

I WASN'T certain what I had done in my life to deserve Rune being in love with me, but I was grateful for it. It was unfathomable that he reciprocated my feelings. I couldn't believe I had been bold enough to kiss him, or that he seemed to enjoy it. The memory of it filled me with fluttery butterflies taking off in a million different directions at once.

Watching Rune cook was like witnessing an elegant dance. Every action was precise and confident as he prepared dinner. Not to mention it smelled *amazing*. I was salivating by the time we sat down to eat our primavera stuffed chicken with angel hair pasta in an alfredo sauce, topped with parmesan shavings.

The dish was gorgeous, with a colorful array of thinly cut zucchini, tomatoes, bell peppers, and red onions tucked into sliced rows in the chicken breast.

Combined with the seasoning and the creamy sauce, it was so good that it was hard not to squirm in my seat. "Rune, this is incredible!"

"I'm thrilled you like it."

"No, I *love* it!" I sighed in contentment as I ate another bite. "Augie would, too. He does most of the cooking at our house."

"I'd be happy to share the recipe."

"Really?"

A hint of a smile tugged at the corner of his lips. "Sure. It's not a state secret or anything."

"Did Renée teach you how to make this?"

He shook his head. "No, this is one of my mom's dishes. She only knows how to cook like six things, but she does those six things very well."

"You could start a restaurant someday. You'd have a queue around the block of customers waiting to get in for this."

"Cooking is how I unwind from stress," Rune explained. "Turning that into a career where I have to do it all the time and yell at chefs on the line every night would ruin that."

It seemed so obvious I regretted my comment. "Oh, that makes sense. I can't imagine you shouting."

"I've always been of the mindset that if you have to raise your voice, you've already lost the fight. Nothing ever gets fixed by screaming at someone."

That was a huge relief to hear. "Da shouted at us whenever he got effing and blinding drunk, which terrified me. Every time he hollered, I hid until it was over."

An angry storm passed through Rune's expressive eyes. "You have my word I won't do that to you. I don't want you to be afraid of me."

Gratitude bloomed in my heart. "Thank you, that means a lot to me. I didn't realize how much I lived in fear at Da's until I moved in with my brother and didn't have to be scared anymore."

"I'm glad you don't have to live with that now. It sounds like things are better for you here."

I didn't want to think about how sad and lonely my life would be if I had stayed in Dublin. "They are. I love living with Brody and Augie. Plus, this is the first time I've had a group of friends who won't judge me for being who I really am. I also got to meet you. What more could I ask for?"

"You're certainly the best thing that's ever happened to me," Rune said.

"I'm not sure how that's true, but I'm grateful you feel that way."

We continued chatting over our delicious dinner. Afterward, I helped him clean up in the kitchen and put everything away. Once we finished, we returned to his living room to sit on the black couch. I was ecstatic that he let me curl up next to him.

But I also wished I possessed the confidence to straddle myself over him and kiss him like I had dreamed about. However, due to my inexperience, the odds I would embarrass myself in front of him were astronomically high. The last thing I wanted was for him to get sick of me because I was clueless about kissing and sex.

"What's wrong?" Rune asked.

"Nothing."

"You keep tensing up."

It was impossible for me to express my concern without appearing painfully young. "What if I'm bad at everything?"

He shifted our positions so he could lift my chin up to meet my gaze. "Luckily for you, you have a very talented and patient teacher." When I tried to protest, he kissed me into silence. I melted when he sucked on my lower lip, then continued kissing me until I forgot what my protests were about. "See? You're a natural."

"I don't know if I would go *that* far."

He caressed my cheek. "I'll always do things at your pace, Callum. I never want to do anything you don't want. We'll take it slow, okay?"

"Won't you get bored waiting?"

"You're worth the wait." The love in his eyes overwhelmed me. "I've waited thirty years for you to come into my life. I can wait a little longer for you to grow comfortable with everything. You don't need to rush into sex because you think that's what will make me happy. You being mine is more than enough."

"I want to—I want to do stuff." My cheeks were flame red with embarrassment. I was unaccustomed to talking about my desires, or even being able to accept that I had them. "But—"

He interrupted me to insist, "I'm serious. If you're not comfortable, nothing has to happen. If I do something you thought you wanted and you change your mind, tell me to stop, and I will. I won't get upset or judge you for not liking it. If you aren't enjoying it, then neither am I."

"Okay."

"I mean it, Callum. It would devastate me if you did something you were uncomfortable with to be with me. I wouldn't be able to forgive myself if I pushed you into something you were too scared to refuse. Please be honest and tell me. I never want to hurt you."

"I promise."

True to his word, he held me and didn't push for anything. I enjoyed the comfort of his embrace, basking in the bliss of knowing he was officially my Rune now.

WHILE I COULD HAVE CUDDLED with Rune all night, he drove me back home after we finished his out-of-this-world good cannoli cheesecake. He had given me extra slices to bring back for Brody, Augie, and myself. I was glad to have another chance to enjoy the pleasure of his fast and sexy car. When we parked in Brody's driveway, I wanted to crawl over the center console into Rune's lap and kiss him senseless. But knowing I was about to introduce him to my family, I behaved myself.

With the container of cheesecake in hand, I let us inside and entered the living room. Unsure what to expect, I made introductions. "Rune, this is my brother, Brody, and his boyfriend, Augie."

"It's nice to meet you both." He reached out so they could shake hands.

"Thanks for bringing Cally home," Brody said. "I hope you had fun tonight."

"It was the best!" I gushed. "Dinner was amazing. And he brought you some of his incredible cannoli cheesecake. I'll go put this in the fridge for later."

On my way to the kitchen, I heard Augie exclaim, "Oh, I never thought about turning a cannoli into cheesecake, but that sounds delicious!"

As I came back, Rune reached into his pocket and pulled out his wallet. He took out a folded-up sheet of paper and handed it to him. "Callum mentioned you might appreciate the recipes for it and dinner, so I wrote them down for you."

Augie accepted it, taking a moment to study it. "Wow, thank you! This looks amazing. Also, your handwriting is *really* nice." He showed it to Brody.

"Impressive. The nuns at our Catholic school would've loved you."

Rune flushed a little under the praise. "Thanks.

My mom didn't want me and my brother to end up with our dad's illegible writing, so she made it a point to teach us good penmanship."

"How terrible is his writing that she went that far?" Augie asked with a laugh.

"She's not wrong when she says he makes a doctor's scribbles look like wedding invitation calligraphy."

Everyone laughed at the description. "Damn, I can only imagine how bad that must be. I appreciate the recipes, though. I enjoy trying new things."

"And I love benefiting from that," Brody added, wrapping his arm around Augie to hug him.

"I'm always happy to chat about cooking," Rune said. "I only ever talk to Renée about it, but she's usually too busy with the restaurant these days."

"Yeah, I've been dying to go to Ambrosia, but the waiting list is almost three years long." Augie wagged his finger at me as he admonished me. "I'm still bummed you didn't take pictures of your lunch when you went there."

He was teasing, but I regretted not doing that. "I'm sorry I got too caught up in the moment."

"If you ever want to go there, let me know," Rune offered. "Getting inside the restaurant may be tricky because of the reservations, but they save the garden for special guests. Maria would be more than happy to host you."

"Wait, are you serious?"

At the same time, Brody protested, "That's kind, but we don't want to use you like that."

Rune waved away the concern. "It's not using me at all. Trust me, Maria and Renée were ready to adopt Callum. He has a standing invitation whenever he wants at this point."

Augie grew excited. "Could I meet Renée?"

"As long as the kitchen isn't swamped, she likes to visit the garden to talk with their special guests. She's great, but she can be a bit of a ball-buster once you get to know her. One of her favorite hobbies is teasing my brother."

"I've been such a fan of hers since I saw her episode of *Chef's Table*," Augie said. "I promise I won't fangirl too hard in front of her."

"She enjoys having her ego stroked, so a little fangirling would go a long way with her, actually."

It had been so much fun meeting them that day. "They were so nice!"

Rune took his wallet out again and handed his business card to Augie. "Let me know when you want to go, and I'll make it happen. If you're interested in exchanging recipes or techniques, feel free to reach out."

"Are you sure it's not an imposition?"

"I would genuinely enjoy it. That's my personal contact information, so it comes straight to me." My heart swelled with love for him for being so nice to Augie. It would be wonderful if they became friends.

"Thank you so much, Rune!"

"You just made his night," Brody joked.

"Only my night? Try my whole damn week is more like it. Maybe even my month. You better step it up if you want to compete."

My brother merely laughed.

"I'm glad, but I should get going since it's late."

Brody shook Rune's hand one more time before he left. "Thanks for stopping by. You're welcome over anytime."

"Is it okay if I email you tomorrow?" Augie asked.

"That would be great. Have a wonderful rest of the night."

After a few more parting words, I walked Rune outside to his car, standing with my back to the house. In the moonlight, he was even more beautiful in his three-piece suit and gold-and-purple marble tie. Now that I knew he was a model, his impeccable fashion sense made so much more sense. "I can't thank you enough for today."

"I'm the one who should say thanks. You've already given me so much."

"But I haven't done anything," I protested.

His warm smile turned my insides to mush as he cupped my face in his hands. "You're you. Loving you is everything to me. My world is a better place because you're in it."

He bent down and kissed me, making me weak in the knees as he reduced me to a puddle. I held on to him for support, light-headed from the rush of happiness flooding through me. If a simple kiss on the lips was this incredible, I wasn't confident I would survive what came next. "I'm still so afraid I'll wake up and find out this is all a dream."

Rune wrapped me up in his embrace, taking away my doubts. I relaxed against him as I returned the hug, feeling safe in his arms. It once again gave me the strange urge to become one with him by curling up in his soul to stay there forever. With my ear pressed against his chest, his voice was a pleasing rumble. "It's no dream."

I knew he needed to go, but I wasn't ready to give him up yet. My need for more made me bold enough to reach up and guide him down for another kiss. He obliged me, the sweetness of it filling me up inside with warm affection for the amazing man I called my boyfriend now.

"Good night, Callum." As always, hearing him say my name sent a tingle down my spine. He placed a tender, lingering kiss on my forehead before stepping away and opening his door. "I love you, and I'll see you soon."

"Love you, too. Night."

He got into his car, and I waited until his taillights disappeared before heading back inside. When I returned, Augie and Brody both had a slice of Rune's cannoli cheesecake. Their matching grins made me self-conscious. "What?"

"You guys are cute together," Augie answered. "It's great he feels the same way about you."

I tilted my head in confusion. "How can you tell?"

"It's obvious."

Brody snorted in amusement. "It has nothing to do with you peeking out the window to spy on them kissing, right?"

"Hey, don't act like you weren't beside me!"

"Sorry." My cheeks flushed over being caught. "Um, well, the thing is…"

"You're not in trouble. I'm happy everything worked out between you."

"I think it's sweet," Augie added. "He obviously adores you."

It reassured me hearing that coming from someone else. "He said he loves me."

"I believe him."

My brother agreed. "I do, too. Anyone who looks at you like that is genuinely in love with you, and not just on a conquest."

All I could do was beam with joy at how everything turned out.

"And my god, can that man *cook*. This is the best thing I've ever put in my mouth." Augie moaned as he enjoyed another bite of cheesecake.

Brody pretended to look miffed. "I'll try not to be offended by that comment."

"Hey, I told you to step it up before. That's on you."

"We'll talk about this later."

"Oh, you can count on it." Augie turned his attention to me and asked, "Will it bother you if I email him tomorrow? I was thinking of sending him one of my recipes to thank him, but I won't if you're uncomfortable with it."

"No, I'm fine with it. He enjoys cooking, so I'm confident he would appreciate it." I held back a yawn, overcome by tiredness now that the excitement had worn off. "Anyway, I'm off to bed. Good night."

After a round of hugs, I headed upstairs. Given the low point I had started on that morning, I was ending the day on an epic high. I couldn't wait to sleep so I could dream about Rune.

Chapter Twelve

RUNE

PRIOR TO CALLUM, I had one boyfriend in my past from freshman year of college. Gui had been a graduate student in the History Department, who was a teaching assistant in my French class. He was the first person I had slept with, which I stupidly assumed made him my boyfriend. I didn't find out until later that I was the only one who thought we were dating. It had been exciting hooking up with someone who was older and that attractive, but I had been too naïve to notice all the red flags.

Gui had been controlling and manipulative, often lashing out at me whenever I displeased him. He never wanted to be seen with me, because he would have been in trouble with the school for breaking the rules by dating his student. I was his dirty little secret, but I had convinced myself that the forbidden nature of our relationship was part of the appeal of being with him.

Everything had been about Gui's pleasure. If I didn't get off on that, that was my problem. Sex had always hurt with him, but back then, I thought that was what being the bottom involved. He never let me take control because he claimed I was too young to know what I was doing. His pattern of abuse was to dismiss every concern I had, without listening to my side of things.

Three months into the relationship, I walked in on him fucking another man. Instead of being repentant for cheating on me, he brought me in the middle and said that was my reward for pleasing him. He told me he had been getting the guy ready for me, and I had been dumb enough to want to believe him. That was the night I discovered I preferred topping.

I stayed with Gui after that, but when I caught him fucking a woman a month later, I ended things between us. He had begged for one more chance, but once I made up my mind, nothing could convince me to change it. After that, I swore I would never have another boyfriend or bottom for someone again.

The weirdest part was realizing afterward that leaving Gui didn't break my heart. It pissed me off he cheated, but I never had a pang of regret after it was over. It had been a relief not being subjected to his emotional whims and rough, unsatisfying sex anymore.

Once I realized I hadn't loved with my first

boyfriend, I concluded something was broken inside me that rendered me incapable of loving someone. It didn't bother me, because casual fucking was best when emotions weren't involved. Everything was easier when you didn't care.

But Callum had changed all that. I wanted to shower him with love and affection, which I had assumed I was incapable of showing anyone. Holding and cuddling him fulfilled me to the core of my soul, instead of making me want to sneak out the second he turned away. It wasn't about chasing after instant gratification. I savored things I hadn't appreciated when I was with Gui, like my first kiss.

With Callum nestled at my side as we watched a documentary about women in the French Revolution, I discovered a new level of happiness existed. It blew my mind that he'd found the documentary himself and asked if we could watch it together. I knew more than it covered, but listening to his excited reactions was an absolute delight. I was a firm believer that not every thought needed to be expressed out loud during movies, but I could have listened to him chatter all night about the program.

When the credits rolled, he couldn't contain his excited reaction. "Wow, that was fantastic!"

"It was quite thorough. Their translations were also excellent, which isn't always the case." It had been a pleasant surprise.

"Thank you for watching it with me. I know it was

probably all review for you, but hopefully it wasn't too boring." His bashfulness was endearing. In his argyle bow tie, black shirt, and jeans, he was adorable beyond compare.

"It's helpful to my future research to see how it's presented." His face brightened with happiness, making my heart swell with affection for him. "Your commentary alone made it worth watching."

"Really? Some people get annoyed when others talk through a movie."

"I'm not one of those people when it comes to you. Please share your running commentary anytime you want. I enjoyed listening to your thoughts."

"Madame de Staël's story sounded so amazing," he said, referring to a woman covered in the documentary. "I think I'll read about her next."

He was in for a treat once he did. "They only scratched the surface of what made her interesting during the Revolution. Her life afterward was equally fascinating. At one point, Napoleon hated her so much that he would punish people by exiling them for meeting her."

"How awful! Why would he do that?"

"Someone once claimed that Napoleon said Madame de Staël 'teaches people to think who had never thought before, or who had forgotten how to think.' He viewed her as a threat." I loved that quote. It was such a powerful thing to do, let alone for a woman to accomplish during the Napoleonic period.

"Did you study Napoleon, too?"

I nodded. "Yeah, I studied what came before and after the French Revolution to understand the full effect of it. You can borrow anything that interests you." To make such an offer was a monumental step for me. Most people treated books carelessly and damaged them, so I never trusted anyone not to fuck up mine. But I knew Callum would treat them with the care they deserved.

"Borrow?"

"Yes, borrow. I'm an academic at heart, which means I'm a hoarder of information. I have every book written in English and French I could get my hands on about those subjects to do my thesis work."

He bounced with excitement at the prospect. "Where?"

"In my office." My apartment resembled a staged home, but my office was my sanctuary that reflected who I really was. It was where I surrounded myself with everything meaningful to me and never let anyone inside.

"Can I see?"

His eager excitement to share the things that mattered most to me warmed my heart. For the first time, I had someone who wanted to share that part of my life with me. It was weird having an unshakeable faith that Callum would appreciate my collection and not make fun of me for owning thousands of books in the digital age. "Sure."

Fancy Love 179

Getting off the couch, I led him to my office. My heart pounded in anticipation as I opened the door and turned on the lights. I turned to watch him enter, and his reaction didn't disappoint.

He gasped in surprise as he marveled at the sight. My black desk sat under the window, with all the walls covered by bookshelves. Stuffed to the gills, they reached up to the ceiling thanks to the shelf extensions I had added. There was a futon in the center of the room for reading and a small bar fridge tucked away under the desk.

Callum stared with the same sense of wonder that a child walking into Santa's Workshop would have. The expansive shelves rendered him speechless, which further endeared him to me. It was gratifying to see the same awe on his face I experienced whenever I entered my office, surrounded by centuries of learning.

"*Wow.*" His gaze darted everywhere, trying to take it all in. "I'm beyond words. Just *wow.*"

I remained silent as I continued observing him explore the room. He took his time as he surveyed everything. Sometimes he would reach out to pet a book, powerless to resist touching their spines. It spoke volumes to me about his love for them, giving me an unexpected bond of kinship with him. I had been the weird kid who would find a novel on the wrong shelf at a bookstore and feel compelled to return it to its rightful home. My parents used to shake their heads at my strange habit, because they never grasped my connection to reading.

It was enthralling watching him peruse the shelves, occasionally pulling a book out to read the back cover. I couldn't believe how many times he chose one of my favorites to check. He was so careful putting them back, taking great care to not bend any corners of the covers or pages. It made me love him even more.

I ached to hold him and thank him for understanding me like nobody else. But that would mean interrupting his experience, and I wanted him to enjoy himself to the fullest. We could have stayed there all night as far as I was concerned.

He eventually commented in hushed amazement, "I feel like Belle in Beast's library. If I lived here, I'd never want to leave again."

His words gave me a mental image of the two of us sitting on my futon together, with him stretched out and resting his head on my lap as we read in companionable silence. With my free hand, I'd stroke his hair, with the only sound between us being the turning of the pages. Afterward, I'd make lunch, and we'd talk about what we read.

Callum saying my name stirred me from my heavenly daydream. Caught off guard by my emotional enlightenment, the best I could manage was to hum, "Hmm?"

"The next time I come over, could we read together?" My heart stuttered as he said out loud what I had been imagining. "I mean, you don't have to read to me, but can we read books at the same time? Or is that too weird?"

I closed the distance between us and gathered him into a crushing hug. How did he know that was what I wanted? Why did he want the same thing? What had I done to deserve the love of someone who understood my soul in a way no one else ever had?

It was a struggle to stay in control of the overwhelming rush of feelings I had for him. "I love you so much, Callum."

"Mm, I love you, too." He rubbed my back in silent comfort. "Is that a yes?"

The trace of hopefulness in his voice moved me to kiss him with heated passion. I couldn't resist sliding my tongue into his mouth when he opened for me. He clung to me as he kissed back, responding with surprising surety.

We were both breathless when I stopped. "It's a yes. Whenever you want to, as many times as you want to, I will always want to read with you."

His bright smile lit me up inside, and I welcomed another hug from him. When he was careful to keep some distance between our bodies, I drew him closer. It excited me to feel his hardness pressing against me. Just when I thought things couldn't get any better, they did.

"I—I'm sorry, it's you, and the kiss, and the books, and *wow* that kiss, and—"

He tried to scramble away, but I held tight and crooked my finger to tilt his chin up to look at me. "Do you want to do more than kiss?"

He squeaked in surprise but stopped trying to leave. It took him several attempts to ask, "Like what?"

"If you wanted me to, I could caress you everywhere while I pleasure you with my mouth." He didn't answer, so I added, "This is up to you, Callum. I'm not pressuring you for anything. All you need to say is no, and I'll stop. I won't be upset with you."

When he pulled back, I let him step out of my arms. He drew a steadying breath, then reached up with trembling fingers to undo the knot of his bow tie. I had no idea that could be so erotic.

He moved on to the buttons of his shirt with fumbling fingers. It was a slow striptease, but also tantalizing. I was as hard as a diamond and dying to touch him, but I refused to rush him.

When his black shirt opened, I admired the expanse of smooth, pale skin. Everything in me wanted to peel that fabric off him and shower him in kisses, but I bided my time.

He looked down to pop the cufflink buttons on his sleeves. His voice sounded a little shaky as he apologized, "I'm sorry that I'm scrawny when—"

I said his name to interrupt him, causing him to

worry his lower lip with his teeth. "You never have to apologize for who you are. You're perfect, just the way you are."

"But I saw the pictures of you online. You have a perfect body, and I—"

I stepped close enough to him to cup his face in my palms as I finished his sentence for him. "And you do, too."

"But—"

"No, no buts. You are by far the most beautiful person I have ever seen, inside and out. Every inch of you is perfect."

He furrowed his brow. "How can you say that when you've worked with so many other gorgeous models?"

"Because not a single one of them can compare to you," I insisted. "Do you need proof of how desirable I find you?"

"Proof?"

"Touch me." When he still didn't understand, I cupped my erection straining in my black slacks. "If you want to, touch me. Find out for yourself how much you turn me on."

He hesitated, before reaching out to check. I covered his hand with mine, pressing it firmly against me. "*Oh*."

I rocked against him, wishing like hell I wasn't wearing pants. "Now do you understand?"

"This is because of me?"

"Yes, because I've never wanted anything more than I want you," I answered. "But I only want what you want. And if this is too overwhelming, we'll stop."

He tugged at his shirttail. "C-could we maybe try the t-touching and the k-k-kissing?"

To start off slow, I ran my hands in tandem up his bare back. My action raised chills on his skin and tightened his nipples into peaks. When I came to his shoulders, I moved to the front and pushed the shirt off them. He shrugged out of it, letting it fall to the floor. "Beautiful."

"Should I take off my jeans?"

I ghosted my fingertips down the curve of his spine, making him shiver. "Only if you're comfortable doing that."

After he kicked his pants aside, it left him in his white briefs, with a faint wet spot from precum. "Would you—I want…I want you to, um…"

"Do you want me to take them off for you?"

He bit his lip again as he nodded.

It was the permission I needed. I reached around and slid my hands down his underwear to squeeze his perfect ass. He inhaled and grabbed my arm to hold on, but didn't stop me. I then hooked my thumbs over the waistband to lower them.

His cock sprung free, and it required every ounce of self-restraint I possessed not to fall to my knees and worship it. I savored the sight of him bare before me, never having seen anything more exquisite. "Absolutely perfect."

I didn't expect him to step forward and start to undo the knot of my black tie with purple roses blooming on it. It stoked the fire burning inside me as he slid it free to drop to the floor. He hesitated before moving on to the buttons of my shirt. "Is this okay?"

"Of course."

Callum undid the buttons on my shirt to reveal my sculpted body. His jaw dropped as he exclaimed, "You actually look like that!"

I chuckled at his reaction as I dropped my shirt. "For the most part. That doesn't stop them from retouching my photos, though."

He reached out and to trace my defined six-pack abs with an appreciative noise. When he tried to undo the button of my jeans, I stopped him. "Are you sure?"

"I want to." There was no hesitation as he eased my pants off my hips to lower them. He reached out but paused. "May I?"

"Your manners are so cute. You don't have to, but yes, you may."

His hand trembled as he reached out to touch my arousal through my black briefs. I inhaled when he caressed me, which felt a million times better without the restrictive pants interfering. "Bloody hell, you're *huge*."

I couldn't hold back my arrogant smirk at his awed reaction.

"Um, you were right before."

Too aroused to follow his thought process, I requested, "I need you to be a little more specific than that."

"When we were texting before your business trip. You told me I had virgin eyes because I'd never seen a prick that wasn't my own."

"I did say that." My response made him grin. "You're allowed to ignore it. Or, if you would rather explore without doing anything sexual, that's fine, too."

"What, you mean just look at it?"

He sounded so scandalized it was a challenge not to laugh. "Sure. You're free to look and touch without getting me off."

"That's not weird?"

"Not at all." I led him over to the futon that was still folded out into a bed from the last time I had read in my office. As much as I ached for gratification, it was more important to me that he was comfortable. He deserved better than I got from Gui. I had barely seen his dick before he shoved it inside me with minimal preparation.

He mimicked my actions from earlier. It was heaven to have his hands on my ass, and even better when my hard-on broke free from the last of my clothing restraints.

"Jesus, Mary, and Joseph," he swore as he stared at it, all three of the names running together.

I stretched out on the futon with a chuckle, beckoning him to come closer. "I've never heard you take the Lord's name in vain, let alone his entire family."

He sat next to me, still regarding my erection with curiosity. "That's because this is worth blaspheming for."

I reached up and caressed his cheek. "Have I mentioned how much I love your Irish accent? I could listen to you say the word 'blaspheming' all night."

"I'm sure this'll keep me blaspheming right through the morning," he retorted with a laugh. "Look at it."

"You're welcome to. Touch it, stroke it, whatever you're okay with doing."

He ran his fingers along the underside of my length. "You magnificent bastard."

I snickered at the comment. "I'll accept that compliment, thank you."

Callum wrapped his hand around my hardness, which welcomed the attention. "I don't think it'll fit."

"Trust me, it will. But we'll save that for another night, okay?"

"Mm-hmm." He rubbed his thumb over the ridge of my cock, then the head of it. Desire flooded through me, but I steadied myself. "I've never seen someone who's cut before. I like it, though."

He brushed his fingers through my trimmed

pubes. Before he could ask, I told him, "I have to do that for work, but I don't expect you to."

"It's so much neater." He followed my thin happy trail up, then back down again. "Have you ever had to do full frontal before?"

"No, but I've gotten as close as you can with strategically placed items." He hesitated before moving further south, so I encouraged him, "You can keep going."

"Be honest. Am I torturing you?" He didn't wait for my answer before he brushed against my balls.

I rubbed his upper arm in reassurance. "I'm happy you're touching me at all. I told you, I'm good with whatever you're comfortable with."

He gathered my sac in his palm, applying pressure in a way that made me ache for a more substantial touch. I reminded my body that wasn't what this was about.

"Why do you keep reassuring me?" He ran his fingertips along the seam of my balls and back up to my dick again. "Don't get me wrong, I appreciate it. But why are you so insistent?"

"For a few reasons. You're an absolute sweetheart who would do anything to make someone happy. I don't want that turned against you by making you feel obligated to do something for me sexually, because you're afraid you'll disappoint me if you don't agree."

He smiled wanly as he shifted on the bed to study

my torso next. "That sounds like something I would do."

"I repeat it to help you believe that I'm sincere." His fingertips ghosted over me, raising chills on my skin. "It's also because I don't want you to think I only meant it the first time we're together. It is true anytime, even if it's ten years down the road."

He paused in his exploration to look up at me in surprise. "Are you serious?"

"If you say no—"

Callum interrupted. "No, I understand that part. I meant, are you serious about the ten years thing?"

"Yes, and beyond." I had no doubts in my mind about it. "This isn't a fling for me, where I'll use you and dump you once the thrill of the chase disappears. You're it for me."

"What do you mean?"

I sat up to face him. "I mean you're my one and only. Before you, I thought true love was a myth, but I love you with all that I am, Callum. Nothing will change that. I want to read books with you, and wake up to your smile every day, and make you chocolate chip pancakes with whipped cream in the morning. I don't just want you in my life. I *need* you in my life. You're my heart and soul."

He hugged me so hard it almost knocked the wind out of me. "How did you know chocolate chip pancakes and whipped cream are my favorite?"

"I had a hunch." It gratified me to know I was right about that.

He kissed me, making me melt for him all over again. "I feel the same way about you, but I was afraid it was too soon."

"That's another reason I'm fine with taking it slow. We have the rest of our lives together. There's no need to rush right now. I know how awful it is being pressured into doing things you aren't comfortable with, because you can't say no without losing that person. The last thing I want is for you to feel powerless."

"Did someone do that to you?"

"Yeah, the first guy I was with." I wished I didn't have to ruin the moment by talking about Gui, but it was important. "I never loved him, though. You're the only one, Callum. Now and always."

His eyes held so much sympathy that it helped heal the old hurt. "What happened?"

"He was significantly older than me, so he constantly talked down to me for being so inexperienced. I'll spare you the specifics, but suffice it to say, if I said 'No,' he kept going. I couldn't tell him I didn't want to do something, because he'd remind me how easy I was to replace. I did everything he demanded, and he cheated on me, anyway."

Tears welled up in Callum's eyes. "I'm so sorry."

I stroked his soft hair, reassuring both of us with my action. "He was out for his pleasure only, and he always hurt me to get it. I would never forgive myself if I made you feel that way. That's why I keep checking in with you."

Callum dabbed at the tears that had gathered. "You have my word. I promise I'll let you know if I'm not okay."

A weight lifted off my chest. "Thank you. That goes for things outside of sex, too. If I suggest we vacation in Hawaii, and you hate the idea because your fair skin will turn you into a lobster in five minutes, please let me know."

He laughed, lightening the mood again. "In that case, I'll tell you now—I *hate* skiing. I've never been, but I'm terrified of going downhill on two thin planks of fiberglass."

"Good, that makes two of us." Filled with gratitude, I kissed him hard.

He moaned into it and lowered onto the bed with me over him. "I think I would like the touching and kissing part now."

I was all too happy to oblige. It was fun taking my time to worship him with my lips and reverent touches that raised chills on his skin. When I reached his nipple, I lapped at it with my tongue until it hardened into a nub. He jolted under me when I sucked on it. Pleased with the response, I kissed my way over to the other one and mirrored my actions before moving further south. He giggled when I neared his stomach.

"Ticklish?"

"Yes, but please don't," he requested, still laughing.

"Okay." Small as it was, hearing him set a boundary eased my fears. I ran my fingers through his nest of dark auburn hair, stopping short of temptation.

Before I could ask for permission, he lifted his hips as he pleaded, "Please."

I kept my touch light and teasing as I toyed with his rigid length, enjoying the buildup of anticipation.

"How did you survive me exploring you? This is torture."

"Does that mean you'd prefer me to use my mouth instead?"

"Yes!" He backtracked in his embarrassment from being overeager. "Um, that is, as long as it's okay?"

Not needing to be told twice, I readjusted my position so I could go down on him. I relished his shocked gasp as I teased his member with my tongue, before sucking on just the tip. Not wanting to overwhelm him, I slowly let him slide into my mouth before pulling off and then taking all of him in again. I moaned around his length when he gripped my hair.

Satisfied he had the idea, I worked on blowing him in earnest, careful to hold his hips down so he wouldn't gag me. "Oh, *god*! Rune! *Rune!*"

The sound of him crying out my name was like hearing the best symphony in the world playing my favorite song. I rewarded him by swallowing around him. That earned me a pleasing shout. "Fucking fuck! *Ah! Fuck!*"

Never having heard him use any iteration of the word "fuck" before, I got a weird thrill out of pushing polite Callum to the point of swearing. He tensed up under me, his fractured sound of pleasure getting more frantic as he neared his peak. I deep-throated him with a hum, resulting in him arching up and shooting down my throat with a loud, wordless cry. Nothing tasted better than Callum's enjoyment. I licked my lips to catch every salty drop of him.

He trembled from the strength of his release with a satisfied moan since words were beyond him. That was fine with me.

I lay down next to him, content with ensuring he had enjoyed his first blow job. "Feeling good?"

Callum's answer was a groan I knew translated into *yes*. I watched him come down from his high, not liking when his anxiety appeared.

"Sorry, I shouldn't have—in your mouth." His cheeks burned with embarrassment.

It amused me he couldn't bring himself to say "come." I reassured him, "You don't have to apologize. I wanted you to do that."

"You did?"

"Tasting your pleasure is the best delicacy of all."

He scrunched his nose adorably. "You like the taste?"

"I do. It's okay if you don't, though."

"Maybe I'll try another day," he said with a tired laugh. "Wait, you haven't come yet."

"No, but that's fine."

He struggled to sit up and stare me down. "That is *not* fine."

"This was about you tonight," I reminded him.

His flare of indignation aroused me. "If it's only about my pleasure, then I'm no better than the first guy you were with. Yours matters, too!"

Damn, he had me there. I never tired of seeing him getting riled up defending me, even if it was against me. His fiery spark excited me on many levels. "No, it's—"

"I want to wank you," he interrupted in a rush of words, before remembering to tack on, "please. I might be bad at it, but may I try? Please?"

It took effort not to comment about only if he was certain. He had promised me he would tell me his limits, and I needed to trust him. I rolled onto my back so he could do as he pleased, my erection perking up at the promise of an imminent release. "I'd enjoy that."

Callum repositioned himself, grasping my shaft with more confidence than I expected. He started off slow, trying to find a rhythm. "This feels so different without a foreskin."

"It's the same basic mechanics. I won't break."

He picked up on my cue, tightening his grip as he worked my length with a little more vigor. With him touching me, it wouldn't take much to send me over the brink. It was even better doing it in my office, a place where I never expected that kind of pleasure from someone.

"I keep thinking about this inside me." He moaned, which shoved me to the precipice of my climax. "You're going to teach me all new ways of blaspheming with it, aren't ye?"

His voice saying those words sent me over the edge. I called out his name as I came, spurting all over him and my stomach. Getting off from a hand job had never felt so great.

"Wow, you weren't kidding about my accent, were you? I say the word 'blaspheming' and you went off like a popper. Incredible!" He tentatively licked some of my cum off his hand.

If it was possible to come again so soon, I would have. When he did it again, I groaned, "You're fucking killing me, you know that?"

His cheeky grin was too cute for words. I claimed his mouth as mine, delving in for a taste of myself on him. It was divine. When we parted, I gestured for him to lie down beside me.

"But what about the mess?"

"We'll clean up soon. Come here."

To my amusement, he sprawled out on top of me with a content murmur. It turned out the only thing I liked more than hugging Callum was cuddling after satisfying him. Surrounded by my books with the man

I loved in my arms, I had everything I could ever want, because he was everything to me.

Chapter Thirteen

CALLUM

OVER THE PAST THREE WEEKS, Rune had awoken so many unknown things inside of me. With great care, he had taken his time in introducing me to pleasure. He treated me as if I was the single most precious thing in the world, worshipping me with tenderness.

But he always stopped short of what I wanted most. It filled me with a blinding need for more, but he distracted me with other forms of enjoyment until I came. He was so intuitive with giving me what I desired, but he refused to penetrate me. My frustration over wanting more was at war with my embarrassment at begging him to take me. But after almost a month of temptation, I realized he wouldn't do it out of fear of rushing me into something I might not be sure about. It was sweet, but it also drove me mad.

After enjoying his delicious butternut squash

gorgonzola raviolis in a sage brown butter sauce with toasted hazelnuts for dinner, we read on the futon in his office. An undercurrent of need skittered through me and kept me restless. It took time to build up my courage, despite knowing Rune would do anything for me. I had even worn my fanciest bow tie for the special occasion, the blue one Rhys had given me with pink rhinestones.

Taking a private moment to give myself a pep talk in the bathroom, I returned to Rune's office. Instead of nestling against him like I had been before, I straddled myself over his lap.

He lowered his book with an amused look. "Yes?"

Without preamble, I launched into the speech I had practiced over the past few days. "I have four requests."

"What are they?"

"May I please spend the night? I have permission—well, not *permission*, because Brody said I didn't need that at my age—but I have his blessing to stay here tonight. And any other night I want."

Rune set his book aside, allowing him to wrap his arms around me. "You have an open invitation for whenever and however long you wish."

I celebrated my first victory with a chaste kiss. "Thank you. That leads to my second request. Would you please make me chocolate chip pancakes in the morning with whipped cream? Ever since you mentioned it, it's all I can think about."

"*All* you can think about?" he repeated with emphasis.

"*Almost* all I can think about."

He chuckled at my amendment. "I'll make as many as you want."

"You're so good to me." I had to be the luckiest bloke alive.

"What's your third wish I can grant?"

"You sound like a genie when you phrase it that way." It was silly, but he kind of was since he made all my wishes come true.

His blue eyes were bright with amusement. "There's a dirty joke in there somewhere about having you rub my magic lamp."

We both laughed, but my nervousness returned over my third ask. "Would you—I mean, could we—that is, I'd appreciate if we could, um…" It irritated me I was cocking things up after rehearsing it so many times in my head. "I want you to—*Iwanttofeelyouinside-mepleasetakemeIcantwaitanymoreplease*." On the upside, I had verbalized my desires. On the downside, my demand came out as one rushed word. *Bollocks*.

A grin tugged at the corner of his lips. "Even in a jumble of words, you got 'please' in there twice. You really do have the cutest manners."

"*Please?*"

"Only if you say it clearly."

With an annoyed growl, I told myself to get over it. I was a grown man; it should not take such a considerable effort to demand what I craved. "I don't want to stop anymore. And I—I want you to come inside me, and—"

Before I could finish my sentence, Rune ravished my mouth. I moaned as I looped my arms behind his neck, enjoying him taking control. I didn't notice him adjusting our positions until he held me as he stood up. Without thinking, I wrapped my legs around his waist as he walked us into his bedroom.

"Jesus, Mary, and Joseph," I breathed in awe, impressed and turned on by the display of strength.

His room was decorated with black furniture, and the biggest bed I had ever seen dominated the space. The duvet cover was black with red velvet piping, which broadcasted sinful lust. It was beautiful decor, but the room was as impersonal as the rest of his apartment, devoid of any trace of Rune's presence. I understood why we always stayed in his library that made up his heart.

Our reflection in a nearby mirror caused me to laugh when I saw how I clung onto him. "I look like a koala who climbed a tree!"

He snickered as he repositioned me on the bed. In my eagerness, I stripped out of my clothes as fast as I could.

Rune waited until I was bare before he started his striptease. He undid the knot of his pink tie with silver flowers, before unbuttoning his white shirt. When it hit the floor, he put on a show of caressing himself as his hands moved south. My breathing became shaky as he swayed his hips to slide his pants down to kick them aside. He removed his briefs, revealing his impressive hardness. I had to grip mine as I struggled to control myself.

He gestured for me to scoot toward the center. The black-and-red duvet was so soft I got sidetracked by how luxurious it was and that it smelled like him. My attention refocused as he crawled on all fours, making me lie back as he pinned me in place. His member rested hot and heavy against me, sending shudders of lust through me.

Rune kissed up my chest and neck, not stopping until he reached my right earlobe. Once he discovered that was an erogenous area for me, he used it to his advantage by tugging on it with his teeth every time. I whimpered, earning me a chuckle. The sound of his amusement so close to my sensitive ear made me squirm under him.

One of his quirks was a compulsive need to mirror his actions. After he finished on the right side, he did the same thing on the left to avoid playing favoritism. I wasn't sure if he knew that he did it, but I adored that about him.

As he teased me into a frenzy by toying with the shell of my ear, I gripped his massive bicep. I loved how solid he was; he was strong enough to protect me from anything.

"What was your fourth request?"

A nervous squeak escaped from me. "No, it's fine. We can stop at three." I regretted bringing up the fourth and most humiliating option. "Genies only grant three wishes, right? Three is fine. Anything more would be greedy."

"Then be selfish. Ask and it's yours. I'll deny you nothing."

"But it's embarrassing," I muttered, my words fading to a whisper at the end.

His eyes darkened with desire as he looked down at me. "You have nothing to be embarrassed about. Please tell me."

He neared my prick, circling the base without touching it. I tried to move into his touch, but he denied me. It broke down my reserves faster than words could. "You'll laugh at me."

"I won't laugh."

Still throwing up walls, I protested, "I might end up hating it."

"If you do, I'll stop." He had proven many times that he always followed through on that.

"It's shameful, but it keeps happening whenever I imagine us together."

He feathered light touches all over, which both comforted and stimulated me. "If you won't say it, I'll have to guess." I stayed silent, mostly because I was curious to hear his predictions. "Hmm, so what would be something you would find embarrassing to ask for? Do you want spanked?"

I shook my head. "No, that makes me think of nuns punishing kids. It's not sexy for me at all."

"Are you dying to call me Daddy?"

I shoved at his shoulder in mock exasperation. "You're not *that* much older than me."

"Are you interested in role-playing as a student taking a history class with your sexy professor?"

I never knew that was my thing, but my prick twitched at the idea I found *very* appealing. "Um, that actually would be—and with your glasses? Oh, *god*. Yes, I'd *really* love to enroll in that course later, please."

He rewarded me by running his tongue down my sac, before taking my right bollock into his mouth to tease. I grabbed at the sheets with a moan, still *very* aroused by Professor Tourneau teaching me a lesson.

When I thought I couldn't take much more, he pulled back to say, "You could also be a food critic who wrote a negative review of my restaurant. I'd be the chef determined to change your mind about how delicious my desserts were by making you eat one off me."

I almost lost it when I imagined licking whipped cream off Rune's perfect abs. "That sounds *amazing*, but I would never give you a bad review! You're a talented chef—"

He interrupted me by switching his oral attention to my left bollock. After making me keen, he paused to say, "That's why it's role-playing. *You* wouldn't do that, but Mr. O'Rourke from *Foodgasm Magazine* is a different story."

"*Foodgasm?*" I cracked up at the word, in awe of how fast his clever mind came up with witty things. "Okay, I'm definitely in now."

"All right, let's go back to stuff you might *actually* be too ashamed to demand." Damn it, I had almost forgotten about that part of the game. "What about wearing a leash and collar to pretend you're my puppy as I call you 'good boy' and rub your belly?"

The description was so over-the-top I had to laugh. "Absolutely not. Wait, is that real, or are you messing with me?"

"I promise you, that's an actual thing."

If that was the scale I was being judged against, what I was after wasn't so outlandish by comparison. "I'm not into 'good boy,' but I…"

Rune teased my cock to reward me for my progress. "But you want me to call you something."

My voice shook with nerves. "Yes."

"You wouldn't be *this* sheepish asking me to address you by Cally like your family." He continued stroking me as he contemplated options, making me tense up as I teetered on the cliff of my climax. I was so damn close I could barely breathe when he guessed, "Baby?"

The same way it did in my fantasies, hearing him call me that triggered my orgasm. I came hard with a sharp cry, spunk splattering all over my stomach as I trembled from the intensity of it. My reaction baffled me. I covered my face and groaned in humiliation. "Why the fuck does that keep happening?"

Rune shifted positions so he could move my hands away to see me. "Why does that embarrass you?"

"Just because I'm young doesn't mean I'm a *baby*. But every single time I imagine you calling me that, this happens," I complained, gesturing at my cooling seed. "I don't get it! It's infantilizing, and I shouldn't like it!"

"That's not what it's about. A baby is someone cute you want your partner to care for, protect, and love unconditionally as their most important person, right? Being somebody's baby means placing your total trust in your loved one and turning to them for all your needs. It's about having faith they'll be there for you, no matter what."

As I mulled over his words, he had a point. I thought of examples from my daydreams. *I've got you, baby. Baby, you feel so fucking good. I love you, baby.* "It's always when you're reassuring me," I realized with a start. "When you're telling me I'm safe with you, that I'm making you feel good, that you love me."

Rune caressed my cheek with a loving look. "See? It's a single word that sums up how much I love and treasure you, and it shows that my greatest pleasure in life is keeping you safe and happy. Why would that be embarrassing?"

"When you put it like that, the only embarrassing

thing is that I thought it was embarrassing." It amazed me how he had turned that simple word into something so rich with meaning.

"Thank you for telling me, baby."

My body reacted to the term of endearment with a shiver that ran down my spine to my toes. I got lost in him, but my focus sharpened when he brushed against my entrance. I spread my legs further apart to accommodate him. "*Please.*"

Rune got a bottle of lube from his nightstand. I expected him to jump right in, but he covered me in a flurry of kisses and touches. Only after I relaxed did he slide a lubed finger into me. It was painless as he showered me with affection.

He repeated that cycle until he had worked three fingers into me and got me to relax. I was going out of my mind with impatience, wanting him to get to the pleasurable part already.

"Are you sure you don't prefer me to use a condom?"

As soon as things became serious between us, he had gotten tested to show me he was negative for everything. Combined with my need to experience all of him, I had no doubts. "Absolutely positive."

He withdrew his fingers, sending my anticipation soaring. After lining himself up, he paused. "If it hurts, or you need me to stop for any reason—"

"I promise I'll tell you." Perhaps I should have

worried about losing my virginity, but I felt ready after weeks of Rune pleasuring me in other ways.

"Fucking hell," he groaned as he pushed into me. The feeling was more awkward than painful thanks to his thorough preparation. "It's so different."

"What is?"

"I've never done this without a condom." His answer shocked me. "It's *incredible*. Shit, you're so *tight*."

It reassured me that some part of this was his first time, too. I shifted my hips as he sank in to the hilt, filling me. He tried to stay still so I could adjust, but I tightened around his hard length. It earned me a powerful thrust that gave me a glimpse of what was to come. An apology was on his lips, but I demanded, "Oh, *fuck*, do that again. *Please*!" There was too much pleasure for me to be humiliated about swearing.

He did as I requested, causing me to scramble for a hold on his broad shoulders. It was strange having something moving inside me, but I relaxed into the sensation. I had gathered my bearings when he lifted my hips to push in at a different angle.

As blinding pleasure flashed through me, I dug my nails into his skin with a gasp. I became more vocal as his hands caressed me everywhere. His hips drove into me, sending me to new heights of ecstasy I hadn't even known were possible. I was incapable of any thoughts beyond how amazing it felt as my body rocked to the rhythm in search of sensation.

Rune's name was the only word I could remember, and I cried it out as a mantra. My existence became wrapped up in the connection between our bodies, to where I couldn't tell where I stopped and he began. Our souls had merged, bonding me to him forever. He was my everything, and I had never been happier.

Chapter Fourteen

RUNE

I NEVER UNDERSTOOD why sex always left me unsatisfied afterward, despite physically feeling good. Fucking had never been about seeking an emotional connection. I was careful to keep things as distant as possible, which meant my partner either faced away from me or was positioned so they couldn't reach out to me. Someone holding on to me gave me unpleasant flashbacks of Gui pinning me down as he roughly fucked me in search of his own pleasure. It also lent a false sense of intimacy to our actions.

For me, sex released my pent-up sexual frustrations so I could come and get on with the rest of my night. Right before I met Callum, it was little more than a chore I endured hoping that maybe things might not seem so bleak. But it left me hollow and depressed, making me question if I was incapable of true joy or happiness.

Callum saved me from myself. His sunniness chased away all my dark shadows, suffusing me with his warm light and filling that aching void in me. He had been the key to my locked heart that I thought was lost forever, helping me break free from my past.

I hadn't expected there to be such a pronounced difference between sex and being with him. But everything was different and better. With every move, touch, and gesture, I conveyed how much I worshipped and adored him.

He had broken down all my walls. I showed him all that I was because I was his. He didn't embrace me solely with his channel, but with his everything. His legs circled my waist, his arms looped over my neck, his fingers buried in my hair, and his heart was mine. It completed the circuit between us. I wished I could sink into him and be a part of him forever.

While we moved as one, the love I held for him overwhelmed me. His blue eyes may as well have had hearts in them, because his gaze telegraphed loud and clear that he reciprocated my devotion. It was hard not to get swept away by the flood of realizations, but he held on to me, anchoring me in the safest of harbors.

He had shown repeatedly that he accepted me mind, body, heart, and soul. After so many long years of wandering around lost in a haze, I found my home in my other half. He didn't just complete me; he made me a better version of myself.

I couldn't stop touching him as we moved together, letting my fingertips whisper with every caress that I treasured him. Each time he called out my name, it fulfilled me on a soul-deep level. To have the privilege of pleasuring him to the fullest was an unbelievable gift.

As I basked in the glory of being with him, I was attuned to his every need. He tensed as his second orgasm for the night approached. To send him into the highest echelon of sexual ecstasy, I reached between us and sought his renewed hardness. He cried out, squeezing me with his thighs as I pushed him to his limits.

It didn't take much to send him soaring. "Come for me, baby."

His body bowed with the force of his orgasm as he shouted, his cum almost reaching his chest. As I felt his climax ricocheting through him on the most intimate level, I came so hard it was a transcendental experience. Aftershocks jolted through me, setting off extra bursts of ecstasy. I bent down to claim his lips in a gentle kiss, thanking him for all the gifts he had given me. "I love you, baby."

His grip on my hair tightened as he shivered with a satisfied moan. "Love you, too, pet name I have yet to decide on." I couldn't hold back my amused reaction. "Hey, don't laugh! My ability to think right now is about as coherent as smashing letters on a keyboard."

I hated pulling out of him, but I appreciated the debauchery of my cum leaking out of him. "I'm excited to see what you come up with."

He nudged me to lie on the bed so he could sprawl on top of me. It had quickly become his favorite position, and he melted against me with a dreamy sigh when I held him. I stroked his back, causing him to laugh and groan at the same time. "Sorry, but I won't survive a round three, love."

"Love?"

Callum nuzzled against me. "I'm testing it out to see if it works."

"Fair enough."

"You're lucky I'm not calling you 'tiramisu.' I just remembered we have that in the fridge for later," he said. "I really want it, but I also want to stay right here forever and never move again."

"Oh, what a terrible dilemma you find yourself in. Whatever shall you do?"

He propped himself to look at me with a cheeky grin. "You know, you said earlier I could be greedy with my wishes. In theory, I could wish for you to carry me to the kitchen after we clean up so I can have some."

"I have a better idea," I told him.

"As long as I get dessert, I'm willing to consider it."

"If you were so inclined, you could also wish for

me to clean you up and then bring you tiramisu here, so you don't have to move," I suggested.

He lit up with excitement. "Ooh, you're right, your idea is *much* better. May we please do that instead?"

"Your wish is my command, baby." He rolled off me in a fit of giggles. I stole a quick kiss before I got up to take care of myself in the bathroom.

After I finished, I came back with a wet washcloth to clean him off, enjoying any excuse to touch him. It embarrassed him the first few times I had done it, but now he luxuriated under the attention like an indulgent cat.

Satisfied he was clean, I left to make his every wish come true, even the little ones like wanting cake in bed. As I walked down the hall, he called after me, "Please make it a big piece!"

I chuckled at his enthusiasm. It became apparent to me early on that he possessed a second stomach for dessert. I made sure his slice was extra large and got one for me. Callum was generous in spirit with everything *except* dessert. I stacked the dishes on my right arm with silverware and grabbed two bottles of water before returning to my bedroom.

He sat under the covers, propped up on the pillows. His eyes went wide when he saw me enter, making me chuckle. "How do you do that?"

I realized he meant balancing multiple things on

my forearm. "Oh, I worked at a restaurant as a server when I was in high school. Here."

He took the bottle of water first, then the plate and spoon. His adorable wiggle dance of excitement never failed to make me smile.

"Is that enough?" I asked, joining him under the comforter.

"Yes, thank you. I seemed to have worked up quite an appetite thanks to a certain someone." He closed his eyes and sucked on the spoon with a moan as he tried my dessert. "Ohhh, that is *sinfully* delicious. On second thought, this piece might not be big enough."

"There's plenty more if you decide you want another helping. I also made extra for you to take home to Brody and Augie later."

"Thank you." He rested his head on my shoulder and nuzzled against me. "You're so good to me."

I pressed a tender kiss to his forehead. "And you're the best thing that has ever happened to me."

He cooed in happiness as he ate, sounding like a happy dove. "I always wondered if your first time would really be as special as all the movies promise. It couldn't be *that* grand. They had to be exaggerating at least a little, like they do with food."

I wasn't sure I followed. "Do you mean restaurant advertisements?"

He nodded. "Exactly! The commercials always show it as the biggest and juiciest burger ever. But then you order it, and the real thing looks like a charcoal briquette that's been left out in the sun for three days. You know?"

"I'm with you."

"I assumed it would hurt and be awkward because it's me." He savored another bite of dessert. "But because it was you, I forgot to be worried about that."

His comment was heartening to hear. I reached out and stroked his auburn hair. "That's great."

"I didn't expect to find out the movies were actually underselling how special losing your virginity could be." A slight flush graced his cheeks. "I mean, you brought me dessert afterward! I'm pretty sure I win for the best first time."

He was too precious for words. It also made me notice he had almost finished eating. "I feel the same way now."

"Why?"

"Because tonight was my first time, too."

"You mean not using a condom?"

I debated for a moment whether to tell him about what my brother said. However, I owed it to him to be honest about the embarrassing conversation after what he had confessed earlier. "Not only that. Jules had a theory about me."

"You lost me."

"He told me I was a love virgin."

Callum burst into laughter. "Wait, what's a *love virgin*?"

It mollified me he had the same reaction I did. I

waited until he subsided into snickers before explaining. "I had never fallen in love with anyone before, which meant I had only fucked. You're the only person I've ever made love to."

"Seriously?" He scraped the plate for the last morsel of tiramisu left. "Is it that big of a difference?"

"Oh, it's *astronomically* different."

He set aside his empty dish but held on to his spoon. "How?"

"Sex was only about the physical release. Emotions never factored into it for me." It was challenging to verbalize my feelings, but I tried my best for his sake. "But with you, it was a deep, emotional connection in my soul. It was like finally coming home after an eternity of searching for a place I didn't know existed. It was the most profound experience of my entire life to realize that I found myself in you."

"*Wow.*"

I caressed his cheek with a fond look. "Thank you for making my first time special, too." He leaned forward and kissed me, but the sound of his spoon tapping my plate betrayed his ruse. "You're too much, you know that?"

He grinned as he savored his purloined tiramisu. "Can you blame me for being a thief? It's *so* good."

"The joke's on you. I cut mine big enough to share, so you're only taking what's already yours."

"Hey, don't tell me that! It tastes better when it's

stolen." He pretended to pout but couldn't stop from grinning.

I passed my plate over to him, which he accepted with a delighted squeal. "*Bon appétit, mon amour.*"

"That's my sixth wish."

"To French you?" I asked with an arched eyebrow.

"Yes, with your tongue and the language, please."

That was something I would look forward to doing. "Anything for you, *bébé*."

"Tomorrow morning, after pancakes. This is *so* happening." He tempted me by sucking on his spoon. "Could we also do what you mentioned before?"

I needed a second for me to remember what he was referring to. In my defense, there had been a *lot* of pleasure to contend with. "You want me to be your French professor?"

"*Oui*," he replied with a devilish grin. "Don't forget the glasses."

"Wouldn't dream of it." He stacked his plates before relocating to my lap to kiss me senseless. "What happened to you weren't up for a round three?"

"The tiramisu was *really* good, and the French was *super* sexy." He turned my next smart-ass retort into a moan as he pressed his growing hardness against my stomach.

Luckily for me, that was a wish I was happy to grant him as many times as he wanted.

Chapter Fifteen

CALLUM

I AWOKE to Rune holding me against his chest like he didn't want to let go. It was *amazing*. Since he was asleep, I lay still and enjoyed him curled around me, hugging me close. I felt so safe and loved in his embrace. It was the perfect start to the morning after my first time. And it would get even better once he woke up and made us breakfast.

Rune stirred with a soft moan, sending a flash of lust rocketing through me. When he rumbled, "Mornin', baby," my prick stood up at full attention. I held my breath as his hand roamed until he reached the part of me that wanted to be touched the most. "Why am I not surprised you're an early riser?"

My answer came out as a needy keen when he stroked my erection.

"The real question is, do you want me to take my

time pleasuring you, or get instant gratification so you can have breakfast sooner?"

I had to stop him from working me, because it was making it too difficult to think. If I let him satisfy me, the odds of eating in bed because of exhaustion were high. I wanted to watch him cook, so that meant choosing the second option. "You won't take it personally if I choose pancakes?"

He licked along the curve of my ear, before tugging on it. If he kept doing that, we would end up in the kitchen at lightning speed. "Not at all. We'll save the other part for afterward." He grabbed the abandoned bottle of lube from the night before. "Get on top."

I did as he requested but was uncertain about what to do next. "What should I do?"

"Move back a little. There, that's perfect."

"For what?" I asked.

He smirked up at me. "You'll see."

I protested, but he slicked my hardness, then did the same to himself. How was this instant gratification? "What are you doing?"

"Lean down closer, just like that."

Another question was on the tip of my tongue, but I swallowed it when he took both of our pricks in hand and started working them together. The slide of our cocks against each other was unlike anything I had experienced, but I *really* liked it. "Oh, *god*!"

"Nothing like a little blaspheming to start your day off right."

I was too lost in him wanking us both off at the same time to come up with a witty retort. My hips moved of their own accord, thrusting into his grip. Now I understood why he said it would be instant gratification; I wouldn't last long.

He slid his free hand up his chest to play with one of his nipples. I watched as he teased it into a hardened nub, then tweaked it with his fingers. Watching him pleasure himself did it for me, and I came with a gasp. It only took two more strokes for him to do the same. Our cum mingling on his abs made something primal in me purr with satisfaction over marking him as mine.

I braced myself on trembling arms as I bent down for a kiss. "Good morning, love."

"Let's clean up and get you pancakes."

I couldn't wait until every day started that way with Rune.

After we finished, I slid on my briefs. He stopped me before I got my pants, despite having his on.

"Here, wear this."

It baffled me when he held out his white button-down shirt from last night. "Why? It's too big for me."

"Please?"

If he was asking, there had to be some reason I didn't understand. I accepted it and put it on. The sleeves were too long, and it was comically large on my smaller frame. I looked like a young boy trying on his da's clothes. His expression stopped me from joking about it. The desire burning in his eyes was so powerful, it may as well have been a physical caress. He wetted his lips, looking intent on ravishing me.

Rune approached me as a predator tracking its prey. It didn't scare me as much as it exhilarated me. I stood stock-still as my heart raced. When he came near, I trembled in anticipation. He used the shirt to yank me closer, then kissed me with a passionate desire that had me clinging onto him for dear life. He was always so tender, but now he dominated my desires. The fierce need set me alight, making my body burn for his touch.

When he pulled back, I was almost dizzy. Everything in me demanded he strip the shirt off me and claim me with that raw passion. Instead, he acted as if he had done nothing out of the ordinary as he fastened a few of the buttons closed. "Ready to eat?"

"You kiss me like that and then expect me to want *food*? All I want is whatever just happened."

"We'll get to that." His promise sent a thrill through me.

"I'm not sure what 'that' is."

He chuckled as he walked out of the room shirtless, calling out over his shoulder, "Oh, and don't put on pants."

I studied my reflection in the mirror, trying to understand what the hell I had done to inspire his reaction. There were no answers to why a badly fitting shirt earned me one of the most mind-blowing kisses of my life. I looked absurd, but it kind of felt like he was indirectly embracing me through the fabric. After a quick check to make sure he wasn't watching, I held the collar up to my nose and took a deep breath. A moan escaped as his lingering scent stoked the fire inside me to burn hotter. Okay, maybe I understood it a *little*.

TO ME, cooking was a means to an end for getting sustenance. For Rune, it was an art form. He commanded his kitchen like a maestro in front of an orchestra, every move precise and beautiful. It had never occurred to me that making breakfast could be sexy until I saw him preparing food. After the explosion of passion right before, it threw more fuel onto my raging flames of lust. It didn't help that whenever he glanced at me, he looked ready to pounce on me and send the buttons flying. I never knew that appealed to me, but it kept me squirming in my chair as I fought against my arousal.

"Do you like cinnamon?"

I blinked at him several times, as the words processed through my hormonal desires. "Yeah, why?"

"Here, you'll love this." He put a generous helping

of something that looked like brown whipped cream in the center of the pancake stack before handing it over to me.

"Are you telling me you made *cinnamon whipped cream*?"

He grinned at me, then set down the bowl between us as he took a seat next to me on the barstool at his black marble countertop. "That's exactly what I'm saying. Help yourself when you run out."

I cut into the fluffy pancakes, moaning as I savored my first taste. The tiny kick of spice in the cream enhanced the sweetness of the chocolate chips. "Oh, that's fucking *delicious*."

"It must be, because I've never heard you swear over food before." He chuckled at my reaction as he ate.

Words were insufficient for how exquisite it tasted. It surpassed the boundaries of what language expressed. The pancakes were so tasty that I didn't care that it sounded like I was making love to my breakfast as I reacted with vocal delight. I indulged in multiple extra helpings of the cinnamon cream. He was lucky I restrained myself from licking it straight out of the bowl.

Rune watched me with amusement, but that heat from before would return to his eyes when he stared at his shirt slipping down my shoulder. Intrigued, I "accidentally" pushed it off further under the guise of scratching an itch. It earned me an interesting glimpse of his willpower at work in restraining himself from acting on his impulses. It was sweet of him to control himself so I could finish my meal. However, I had the strangest urge to test how far I could push his limits before he caved into his need. I never thought I would be so bold, but his intense reaction left me desperate to discover what happened once he gave in.

Between the incredible breakfast and his beautiful body on display, my arousal came on quick. I took my next-to-last bite with a moan, shifting to draw his attention to my hardened prick peeking out from under his shirt.

His grip on his fork tightened, and he appeared about a nanosecond away from losing control.

I let the moment drag out as his composure slipped. The instant I put the last forkful in my mouth, he swept me off the barstool before I could finish chewing. I held on to him and laughed, entertained and turned on by his caveman reaction.

"You did that deliberately, didn't you?" he asked as he carried me to his bedroom.

"Was it that obvious?"

He grinned, but as soon as he put me down, that predatory prowl returned from before as he embraced me from behind and studied us in his mirror. His hardness pressed against my back as he rubbed my cock between the shirttails. The intense enjoyment I derived from watching Rune reverently kissing my bared shoulder defeated my sense of shame. It was arousing to watch him giving me pleasure in a way I hadn't been able to see before.

I wanted another glimpse at what he had been fighting so hard to hold at bay. It made it easier for me to plead, "Show me."

"Show you what?"

I turned to look up at him with lowered lashes as I tugged the shirt further off my shoulder. "What you want."

He clenched his hands into fists to keep himself from reaching out to me. "You're not scared?"

To answer his question, I undid the first button. He swallowed hard when I reached the next one. "I want to know, Rune. Won't you please show me?"

At my words, the last of his resistance shattered. In an instant, he had my back thrown up against the wall as he caged me in place. His lips claimed mine in a crushing kiss as he pinned my wrists. I gasped, but he didn't stop ravishing my mouth. The taste of cinnamon lingered on his tongue, which heightened my enjoyment further as he obliterated my ability to think of anything other than *fuck me*.

I rocked against his thigh he had forced between my legs, offering just enough resistance to make him push me back harder. While I enjoyed being cherished, being ravaged was also a goddamn delight. I felt like we were acting out his elevator commercial, which was an even bigger turn-on.

We were both breathing heavily by the time he paused. He stared down at me with a dark need that drew me in rather than scared me away. I thrust against his leg again, needing some friction for relief before I lost my mind to lust.

Instead of giving me what I wanted, he undid the last two buttons and stripped off my briefs, before carrying me over to the bed. After removing his pants, he positioned himself on top of me. He drank in the sight of me wearing his shirt, spread out on the sheets. It was the calm before the storm, because he leaned down and kissed me so hard, I forgot what air was.

He sucked on my bottom lip, applying the slightest bit of pressure. It was so different from the other kisses he had given me, but I was into it. I wanted to drown in the taste of his lips on mine, but he set about worshipping me. It was an unbearable slowdown from the fast buildup, which frustrated the hell out of me. Before I could complain, he teased my nipple with his tongue, then used his teeth again to tug on it.

It resulted in an unexpected burst of pleasure. "Do it again." As he mirrored his actions on my other one, I tried to touch myself for some relief, but he knocked my hand aside. An annoyed growl slipped out that startled me. When did I start making those kinds of noises? *Since you want more and he's not giving it to you.*

Rune distracted me by going down on me while stretching me with lubed fingers. He had eased me into my first blow job, but he went straight for deep-throating now. He tormented me by leaving only the tip between his lips, teasing my foreskin, then swallowing me down again. Every time I got close to orgasm, he would back off. He did it several times, working me up into a frenzied need. "Goddamn it, let me come!"

I slapped my hand over my mouth, unable to believe I had said such a rude and demanding thing. He didn't give me the chance to regret it, because he took me all the way in as he stroked that sensitive spot inside me. I cried out as I climaxed, shaking from the intensity of it.

He withdrew and moved away, triggering my remorse. "Sorry, I shouldn't have said—"

"Baby, come here." His words were gentle yet commanding as he crooked his finger and gestured for me to move closer. "I'm not mad, and you're not in trouble. It was sexy as hell. Get over here so I can show you how much I enjoyed it."

Relieved that his actions hadn't been punitive, I positioned myself over him as I had been earlier that morning.

"I want you to ride me with my shirt on. Do you feel comfortable doing that?"

To answer, I slid his lubed cock against my arsecrack. "God, yes."

The embers that had died down sparked in him again, sending excitement racing through my veins.

He instructed, "Ease onto me and remember to breathe. If it hurts, stop and don't force yourself. Okay?"

"I promise." With those words, he helped guide his dick to penetrate me. There was a slight discomfort as I got used to him breaching me from that angle. I relished the fullness, loving how our bodies connected.

His hands gripped my thighs until he realized what he was doing. He rubbed them in silent apology. "Go at your own pace. Don't rush."

I clenched around him, earning me a reflexive hip jerk from him. It took me a few stops and starts to find what worked for me, but Rune stayed patient with me as I fumbled through figuring out the mechanics. Once I found the right rhythm, it progressed from being strange to pleasure in the blink of an eye. It was incredible whenever he pushed up to meet me on a downward bounce. My hands roved over his sculpted abs, further heightening my enjoyment. I discovered very quickly I liked being in control.

While I wasn't a vindictive person by nature, it was fun getting payback from earlier. I sped up and slowed down the same way he had done to me. He struggled to hold back, gripping my arse to help me take him even deeper. The slight roughness of it made me cry out with abandon as I rode him hard.

His hands supported me when my pace got erratic thanks to my renewed arousal. The burning need from earlier returned to his gaze as I hardened. "Let me see you touch yourself."

Without thought, my body reacted to do as he demanded. I wanked off as my hips rocked in search of my second orgasm. As the pleasure overwhelmed me on two fronts again, my pace faltered as it became too much to handle. I grew frustrated when I couldn't find the right angle to send me over the edge. Nothing gave me what I needed. In my irritation, I bounced down hard enough to wince from a flash of pain.

"Easy, easy. Try leaning forward."

Desperate for release, I did as he said and put my hands on the bed for leverage. The change was immediate. I groaned when it allowed him to hit the spot that made my toes curl. A torrent of swears fell out of me as I rocked hard against him while he worked my arousal with a firm grip. "Fucking *fuck*!"

My body moved with a primal desire to get off, frantically pumping my hips as I welcomed him pounding me harder than I ever imagined I would enjoy. I raced toward my peak as I rutted against him with blind need, completely at the mercy of the animalistic urges driving me.

Everything was a flurry of movement as I tensed in anticipation of the tingling running through me. I teetered right on the precipice of the cliff, which he shoved me off of when he ordered, "Come for me, baby."

I shouted as I ejaculated onto his stomach with a full-body shudder.

Rune tugged on his shirt to jerk me down for a harsh kiss, our tongues battling it out. I broke it with another cry as he came inside me with a ferocious growl of his own.

Spent, I couldn't support myself on my shaking arms. I collapsed on him with a satisfied groan, not giving a single shite about the mess between us. I giggled when he snuggled me.

"What's so funny?"

"We went from blind lust to sweet cuddles in less than a second. And we also forgot to pretend you were my professor."

Rune stroked my hair to soothe me. "Sorry, it was too arousing seeing you dwarfed in my shirt to remember we were supposed to be role-playing. I promise we'll do it later, though."

"I'm certainly not complaining. If this is the result, I'll wear your clothes a lot more often."

He hugged me tighter with an amused rumble of laughter. "I can guarantee I'll show you my love and appreciation every time. It's arousing seeing you dwarfed in my shirt."

"Had you thought about it before today?" I asked.

"Too many times to count."

The answer surprised me enough to prop myself up to see him. "Seriously?"

He caressed my hair with a roguish grin. "If you

want to send me over the moon, put on my tie." I stared at him in shock. "Sorry, was that too much?"

"No, I—"

When I cut myself off, he urged me, "You can tell me anything, baby. I won't judge you."

My cheeks flushed as I confessed to him. "I've thought about you wearing one of my Zapfirino bow ties. It's rather…*alluring*."

"That's another wish of yours I can't wait to grant."

His answer encouraged me to be greedy. "Can I push my luck and ask for more pancakes for lunch? I didn't finish all your cinnamon cream yet."

"Anything you want, baby."

He was so good to me. "I want you most of all, love."

"You have me. Now, and always."

He kissed me again, making my heart sing with joy. Who knew bow ties could bring true love into your life?

Epilogue

RUNE

ONE MONTH LATER

WITH CALLUM IN MY LIFE, it had been so long since I had a shitty day that I had almost forgotten how much they sucked. I was too good at my job to get yelled at like a punk by an unprofessional photographer over his fuckup. After the stress of dealing with that bullshit, all I wanted to do was spend an evening with my boyfriend and forget about the world for the night. Unfortunately, he was busy tonight. I would never begrudge him hanging out with his other friends, but it didn't stop me from wishing he was with me instead.

In the elevator, I loosened the knot of my pink tie as my weariness hit me hard. It weighed on me as I waved my key fob over the electric lock to let myself in. I had barely opened it when I froze at the sight of the lights on, which I had shut off that morning. Before my paranoia could kick in that feared an intruder, I heard Callum's voice coming from my kitchen. "Please be perfect! I don't want to be embarrassed."

"Embarrassed about what?"

Callum spun around to face me, lighting up with a bright smile that obliterated my previous irritation. He wore my black apron over his light gray suit, with a lavender plaid bow tie and an aubergine button-down shirt. The domestic scene was pure bliss. "Welcome back, love!"

After years of my apartment being the place where I slept in between work, it had finally become a home with Callum's presence. I walked over to him, my stress melting away as I embraced and kissed him hello. He was too cute in my apron. "I thought you were busy?"

"Yes, busy making you dinner. You sounded like you had an awful day, so when Jules stopped into the office to visit Xander, I asked if he would help me surprise you tonight."

It looked like I owed my brother another thank-you. "Best surprise ever."

"No, the surprise will be if it's edible."

I hugged him from behind as I peered over his shoulder at what was baking. It was chicken breast with mozzarella bubbling on top of it that made my mouth water. "Baby, you could serve me sawdust, and I'd still be thrilled because you cooked it."

He leaned against me, so I held him tighter. "If that's the bar I need to clear, then I might be okay. We're having pancetta-and-mushroom-stuffed chicken breast, with rigatoni alla vodka."

"Mm, it sounds delicious."

"I also tried to make a dessert for the first time, but it'll probably end up being an ambitious disaster, so please don't get your hopes up." Callum moved out of my hold to stir the pasta sauce. He held up the wooden spoon for me to taste it. "Does this taste right?"

The flavor was robust and far too wonderful for him to be so insecure about his abilities. "Better than okay. It's fantastic. You don't give yourself enough credit."

He flushed as he stirred it again. "I'm just following Augie's recipe."

"And you're doing a great job. What's for dessert?"

"If I didn't mess it up, we'll have a spiced peaches panna cotta with raspberry coulis and champagne gelée. I'm worried it won't set in time, though."

His menu impressed me. "If it needs more time, I don't mind waiting. It'll be worth it."

"I know you like Renée's raspberry peach Italian cream soda, so I hoped you would enjoy this, too."

Unable to resist any longer, I gave him an appreciative kiss. "Thanks for being so thoughtful." I was grateful he was meticulous in his prep, keeping my kitchen spotless as he worked. Messy counters stressed me out, and it was a relief to not come home to that. I wished I could carry him to the bedroom and reward him, but I would wait until later. Instead, I observed him as he did his final preparations.

Once he finished, we carried our plates over to my glass dining table and sat across from each other. He watched me cut into the chicken and take my first bite. I gained a new appreciation for why he always reacted to my cooking the way he did. That he had prepared it for me with love made it the most delicious thing I had eaten in my entire life. "Mmm, this is incredible, baby."

He tried his dish, making a surprised noise. "It's actually good!" He did one of his cute happy dances in his chair. "I'm so glad I didn't screw it up! Maybe there's hope for the dessert."

In the end, his panna cotta turned out to be the best I had ever had. It was even better than Renée's drink. Each bite filled me with the joy and satisfaction that being loved by Callum brought me, fulfilling me on a spiritual level. I couldn't wait to show him my appreciation by worshiping every inch of him tonight and forever.

What special present does Rune give Callum for their anniversary? **Claim your copy of Something Blue to find out today**!

The series continues with Jules and Xander's story! Can their fake wedding date lead to true love? **Read Love Fool next to find out what happens**.

Want to see where the Sunnyside universe begins? **Check out Bet on Love to start the adventure**.

Thank You

Thank you for reading **Fancy Love**. Reviews are crucial for helping other readers discover new books to enjoy. If you want to share your love for Rune and Callum, please leave a review. I'd really appreciate it!

Recommending my work to others is also a huge help. Don't hesitate to give this book a shout-out in your favorite book rec group to spread the word.

About the Series

If you want to see more of Callum and Rune's story, you can read an exclusive bonus chapter if you join my newsletter.

They'll also appear again in all the remaining books of this series: **Love Fool**, **Love Directions**, **Picture Love**, and **Love Practice**. Additionally, they have a guest cameo in the first book of my **Suite Dreams** series, **Snowbody Like You**.

The next book in this series is **Love Fool**. It focuses on Rune's older brother, Jules, and his romance with Xander Dandridge, who is Rhys's personal assistant from Chapter 8 of **Bet on Love**. That's the first book in the **Good Bad Idea** series, so consider checking it out to see where the fun begins.

All of Callum's friends from Chapter 8 will tell their stories in upcoming books, so this is only the start of their journey. I know a lot of you were really excited for Felix to get his own story after meeting him in **Love Means More**, so be sure to check out his smoking hot brother's best friend, insta love, age gap, gay romance with Arsène in **Picture Love**.

In the fifth book in the series, **Love Directions**,

North has a very sweet and heartfelt romance with a character you'll meet in the next book. It's a cute and funny insta love, shy/flirt, opposites attract, gay romance.

Wren and Izzy will close out the series with their hilarious romance in **Love Practice**. It's a friends to lovers, roommates, fake dating, gay romance that will have you rolling with laughter.

To stay up to date on the latest series news, please be sure to subscribe to my newsletter, follow me on Twitter and Instagram, or join my Facebook group, Ariella Zoelle's Sunnyside for exclusive weekly teasers. We have really active community, so please come and introduce yourself!

Next in Series

AVAILABLE NOW

Jules has always been willing to do anything for his best friend, Xander. But does that include finally confessing he's been in love with him for years?

Xander Dandridge

Once I dump my dirtbag ex-boyfriend, I'm ready to wash my hands of him. Unfortunately, he's going to my boss's wedding, which means I need a new date ASAP. Like I always do, I turn to my best friend for help because Jules will do absolutely anything for me. As expected, he's more than happy to play the part of my fake boyfriend. It's an especially genius idea since my ex *hated* Jules with the fiery passion of a thousand burning suns. Plus, I might get the added bonus of having some friends-with-benefits fun with Jules to blow off steam after ending my unsatisfying long-term relationship. Major win-win!

There's just one tiny flaw to my masterplan: I wasn't *actually* supposed to fall in love with Jules. It's obviously time for a new strategy. What about trying to turn our fake relationship into a real one?

Jules Tourneau

I'd do anything for my best friend, Xander—including pretending I haven't been madly in love with him since we were kids. When he asks me to be his fake boyfriend, even though I know it's a terrible idea, how could I say no? Especially when I get to tease him with obnoxiously cutesy nicknames while taking care of his *very* real needs to satisfy both of us.

Next in Series 243

It's the best of both worlds as I get to live out my fantasy of openly adoring him in a romantic way.

But once the wedding is over, I'm not ready to give up what we have. I wonder if I can convince Xander to fall in love with me for real?

Love Fool is the fourth book in the ***Good Bad Idea*** series and part of the Sunnyside universe. This novel features a friends to lovers, fake dating, opposites attract, gay romance. If you love cute sweetness, sexy fun, and low angst stories that will make you laugh and swoon, you'll adore this satisfying HEA without cliffhangers. Each book can be read as a standalone or as part of the series in order.

Also by Ariella Zoelle

For a complete and up-to-date list of Ariella Zoelle's low angst releases, please visit her website at

www.ariellazoelle.com/ariella-zoelle-all

Also by A.F. Zoelle

In the mood for something with more angst and drama? Check out A.F. Zoelle's dark romances at

www.ariellazoelle.com/af-zoelle-all

Acknowledgments

It's been a dream come true to see the overwhelming support for this **Good Bad Idea** series. So many of you have shared your thoughts with me about how much you're loving these stories, and that means the world to me. It's been so much fun writing these, so I'm thrilled everyone is enjoying the journey!

A very special thank you goes out to Mona and Taylor for letting me squee so much about this book with them as I worked on it. I'm grateful to have such wonderful friends that celebrate with me.

Almost all of Rune's outfits were inspired by my friend Michael's amazing taste in suits and color coordination. I'm grateful that he always knows how to make me laugh, even when things are at their worst.

I'm so appreciative for the help I've received from Pam, Sandra, and Cate. I couldn't ask for a better team than them, who help make magic possible.

I also want to say thanks to Katie from Gay Romance Reviews and all of the ARC readers who have been so kind and supportive! I truly treasure the fact that so many of you have found these books comforting with all the chaos that's going on in the world right now.

I can't wait to meet again in **Love Fool**!

About the Author

ariella zoelle
WWW.ARIELLAZOELLE.COM

Ariella Zoelle adores steamy, funny, swoony romances where couples are allowed to just be happy. She writes low angst stories full of heat, humor, and heart. But sometimes she's in the mood for something with a bit more angst and drama. If you are too, check out her A.F. Zoelle books.

Get a bonus chapter by using the QR code below!

Printed in Great Britain
by Amazon

43404671R00145